"I hope ... that you can take advantage of me."

"I intend to try."

Helplessly she blinked at him, feeling a slow lethargy creep through her whole body. It must be exhaustion. That would explain the light-headedness, too. She swayed, her lashes dropping over her enormous lagoon-blue eyes.

"Oh, I'm so tired," she mumbled.

"Nice cue," he said in a sexy growl, slowly releasing her. "Time we went to bed, don't you think?" With his gaze locked on hers, he slowly began to undo the buttons of his shirt.

Dear Reader,

We know from your letters that many of you enjoy traveling to foreign locations—especially from the comfort of your favorite chair. Well, sit back, put your feet up and let Harlequin Presents take you on a yearlong tour of Europe. **Postcards from Europe** will feature a special title every month set in one of your favorite European countries, written by one of your favorite Harlequin Presents authors. This month, let us take you to Italy at carnival time, when the streets are filled with music, fire-eaters, dancers—thousands of people in fancy costumes, reveling and celebrating la dolce vita. We want you to join them—to experience romance in a country that has become such a popular destination for lovers!

The Editors

P.S. Don't miss the fascinating facts we've compiled about Italy. You'll find them at the end of the story.

SARA WOOD

WOOD

Mask of Deception

Harlequin Books

TORONTO • NEW YORK • LONDON
AMSTERDAM • PARIS • SYDNEY • HAMBURG
STOCKHOLM • ATHENS • TOKYO • MILAN
MADRID • WARSAW • BUDAPEST • AUCKLAND

With my grateful thanks to
Fulvio Roiter, Anna Setti, Flavia and
Massimilliana for all their help

ISBN 0-373-11628-4

MASK OF DECEPTION

Dear Reader,

Italy is my second home and totally different from
the quiet, remote part of Cornwall where I live with
my husband. With a Welsh mother and a Romani
father, I naturally adore the Italians' love of drama,
their passion for life and all of its pleasures. Researching
Venice meant romantic trips in gondolas, walking
snowy streets at midnight, endless chats with friends
over the best coffee in Europe, and falling madly in
love—with Venice of course!

Enjoy!

Sara Wood

Books by Sara Wood

HARLEQUIN PRESENTS
1302—THREAT OF POSSESSION
1318—LOVE NOT DISHONOUR
1382—NIGHTS OF DESTINY
1414—DESERT HOSTAGE
1470—SICILIAN VENGEANCE
1573—CLOAK OF DARKNESS

HARLEQUIN ROMANCE
2814—PERFUMES OF ARABIA
3066—MASTER OF CASHEL

CHAPTER ONE

'SCUSI. . . Excuse me. . .'

Reluctantly, Meredith dragged her envious gaze from the noisy families greeting one another in the Arrivals lounge and turned to the man who'd spoken. Although she'd been enchanted by the boisterous reunions, her attention was immediately arrested by the man's striking colouring.

Beautifully co-ordinated from top to toe, he wore a soft wool coat that matched eyes as dark as a black Welsh tarn. The elegantly draped silk scarf was two shades paler than his hair. And that, to her surprise, was the colour of unripened corn. Fair and dark. Fascinating.

'Can I help you?' she asked, trying not to let him see the amusement in her blue eyes. For his abrupt switch to English had come after taking one look at her knitted hat, cheap raincoat and brogues. Very un-Italian, he'd evidently decided; this woman must be English! The smile escaped, lighting her face.

'This *is* the flight from London?' he growled softly.

Meredith was disconcerted by his unsmiling reaction because people didn't usually stay immune to her friendly warmth. He spoke in a barely audible, husky growl—but it overlay the rumble of a harshly controlled anger. Intrigued, she moved closer.

'That's right. The schedules are a mess, aren't they? We're over a day late because of the blizzards.' She adjusted the weight of the half-dozen mega-sized carrier bags which contained her clothes, feeling the handles biting into her hands.

The Italian briefly inclined his head, apparently remembering his manners. 'Thank you,' he said curtly. He fiddled with a piece of card he was carrying and glowered at the exit to the Customs hall as if he was expecting his worst enemy to come through the door.

'I don't suppose you're waiting for me?' Meredith asked tentatively, fervently hoping that he wasn't.

'No.' He didn't even look at her.

'Oh. Fine. I thought not,' she said with relief, unabashed by his arrogant dismissal. Someone from the Banco D'Oro was supposed to be meeting her, and this remote blond god certainly didn't look like a bank official—though he might have been Signor Corosini. Her face grew solemn in an instant, and she scanned the almost empty foyer apprehensively, her unpleasant mission remembered.

Blackmail. It was a nasty business. At the very thought of it, her limbs went watery and the carrier bags fell from her numb fingers. Meredith lunged out in a desperate attempt to save their contents only to find her feet slipping on the melted snow which had been walked in from outside.

'*Attenzione!*'

For a second or two she felt the protection of a man's arms holding her securely and then she had crashed on top of him and was lying spread-eagled on a rock-hard body, deceptively concealed beneath soft fabric.

Winded, her face crushed against the soft warmth of his coat, she felt icy breath whispering over her forehead. It must be Mr Fair and Dark, she thought shakily. And, under that air of sheer studied elegance, Mr Fair and Dark was all muscle.

'Oh, goodness, how embarrassing! I'm sorry,' she apologised. Her startled gaze locked with the cold black eyes. 'Your lovely coat. . .'

Her lashes fluttered. The hands had tightened briefly on her arms and the disconcerting eyes, a whisper away, had softened with an alarming, sensual warmth. In confusion she pushed against his chest and awkwardly scrambled off, beginning to pick up her scat-

tered belongings, knowing her face must be a fetching
shade of scarlet.

'Forgive me. . . Will your coat need cleaning?' she
asked anxiously, hoping he wouldn't land her with the
bill. She had enough problems ahead of her, without
worrying about stretching her carefully planned
budget.

'Yes.' Grim-faced, the slow growl of anger in his
voice deeper now, he pushed some of her clothes into
the bags.

Seeing her underwear in a heap, she grabbed at it
hastily. 'Please, I can manage——!' She found herself
having a tug-of-war over her best bra, and felt an
overwhelming impulse to giggle at the silliness of the
situation.

His inscrutable glance met hers and then his heavy
lashes dropped as he released the lacy strap. But he
continued to bundle up her things, nothing in his face
betraying his masculine opinion of the rest of her
serviceable undies.

'Watch your step in future,' he rasped in warning,
standing up and irritably balancing a bag or two against
his leg. He bent to pick up the card he'd been carrying
then scowled at the deserted foyer. 'Were you the last
through Customs?' he demanded imperiously, a frown
marring the smooth gold of his forehead.

'Yes. My case had been destroyed by a rogue
conveyor belt,' she said, wanting to explain her uncon-
ventional luggage. A smile spread over her face as she
recalled the concerned officials, fussing over her like
doting fathers. 'Hence these bags,' she confided. 'The
Customs men gave me a cup of coffee, mopped up my
tears and——'

'*Madonna*!' interrupted the man harshly, bringing
her chatter to a startled halt. 'I wait for nothing!'

'Oh, what rotten luck.' Meredith's sympathetic
understanding didn't register on him at all and, judging
by the malevolent turn to his sensually modelled
mouth, he was absorbed in mentally tearing to shreds

whoever had stood him up. Thank heavens it wasn't her! 'Well, I'd better find the boats for Venice,' she sighed, resigned to the fact that no one had come to meet her.

Collecting together the bulky bags, she had to half drag them along to the exit because they were far too unwieldy for a mere five-foot-one individual to carry. *The bag lady enters Venice*, she thought, trying to cheer herself up for the daunting journey ahead.

'Stop right there!'

Meredith raised an eyebrow at the peremptory order. She turned to see the surly Italian striding purposefully along the snowy jetty towards her. 'Will this take long?' she asked anxiously. 'These bags are in danger of bursting——'

'There aren't any boats. The lagoon's frozen—it's very shallow. You'll have to take a taxi.' He saw her look of dismay and added, 'But don't worry, the canals are OK—you'll still get your gondola ride.'

'Me, in a *taxi*?' she chuckled, ignoring that last sentence. 'Thanks a lot for the information, but girls like me don't take taxis. Can't you tell by the designer hat? This is worn by contenders for first prize in waiting at bus stops.' She smiled ingenuously and the openness of her face seemed to ease his bad temper a little.

'Hang around here at this time of night, and some sex-starved male might decide to make you *his* first prize.' The Italian stared back at her widened lagoon-blue eyes which had become very serious. 'Take a taxi for once. You look as if you need one,' he said gruffly, indicating her bags.

'I can't——'

'Share mine,' he suggested softly.

Meredith hastily curbed her natural friendliness, reminding herself that she wasn't at home now, gossiping to strangers and leaping into any car that came down the lane. She ought to be wary of men like this one. Groomed from his designer haircut to his designer shoes, glossily packaged and undeniably sophisticated, he inhabited another world to that of the men in her Welsh valley.

'You're awfully kind, but no, thanks,' she replied gently, not wanting to offend him. 'I don't know you, do I? I shouldn't even be talking to you. But it's difficult to remember things like that when you've been brought up in a village and you're used to chatting to everyone you meet. My gosh, it's freezing!' She shivered in the icy wind and pulled her warm hat further around her ears.

His eyebrow lifted in surprise. 'You're refusing my offer?'

She smiled. 'I don't imagine that happens to you very often, does it?' Meredith watched the struggle on the man's face as he tried to control his wayward mouth, and wondered why he didn't want to grin when he was so obviously amused by her cheek.

'It's late,' he said evenly, setting his facial muscles into a stiff mask, 'you're cold and probably as tired as I am. We're both going into Venice——'

'But you have someone to meet,' she said, reminding him of his duty.

He gave an indifferent shrug, extracted the piece of card from inside his coat and threw it with a show of distaste into an overflowing rubbish bin. 'The hell I have!' Despite the quietly spoken words, the strong jaw thrust out belligerently. His eyes were so bleak and preoccupied that they failed to register Meredith's surprise. 'I'm damned if I'm going to spend hours of my valuable time meeting every plane that lands. Let the swine skate to Venice for all I care.'

'Sounds as if you've been waiting a long time,' she said soothingly.

'Sure I have. All my life,' he replied in a jaundiced tone.

Meredith grinned at the outrageous exaggeration. 'My, that's a long time!' she chuckled. 'No wonder you're fed up!' She gave him a teasing look, thinking

he'd laugh too. But his scowl deepened and she
sobered a little. 'Maybe,' she continued more gently,
'your friend——'

'Enemy,' he amended, his thinned mouth biting out
the word.

'Oh. Well, whoever.' She felt uncomfortable with
his anger but her sense of fair play drove her on. 'You
know, the weather's terrible in England—wall-to-wall
snowdrifts. Heathrow airport is absolutely chaotic.
Maybe your. . .visitor,' she said carefully, 'is stuck in
a snowdrift——'

'Now that's a pleasing thought,' he said in a vitriolic
drawl.

His expression was inscrutable, but his hands were
clenched so tightly into fists that Meredith marvelled
at the man's ability to keep the muscles of his face so
impassive. She wondered idly what had prompted the
Italian's hatred.

'You don't mean that,' she remonstrated, her own
face showing everything she thought and felt as usual.
And Meredith was troubled. Talking to strangers
might be unwise, but she thought of the ghastly
welcome awaiting the tired, unsuspecting traveller,
and felt sorry for him. 'Please,' she said coaxingly.
'Put yourself in his shoes——'

His mouth twitched. 'I have,' he said sardonically.
'That's the problem. That's why he's here. But I've
got it in hand.'

With unashamed interest, he studied her anxious,
freshly scrubbed face, and she found herself responding to the arrival at last of his faint, elusive smile, her
limpid eyes softening with warmth because she knew
instinctively that he smiled rarely and that she was
privileged.

There was something in the quality of his quiet,
confiding tone that made her feel there was an intimacy
between them. She'd never known a man speak so
softly—or to greater effect. She moved back a step,

after discovering that she'd unknowingly moved closer to him than was socially acceptable.

'I'd better go——' she said awkwardly. 'I was hoping someone would come, but I can't blame them for not waiting all this time. If I can navigate my way around Heathrow airport, I can get to downtown Venice.'

As he opened his mouth in protest, she lifted her hand to stop him and her elbow caught the card which he'd pushed into the bin. In glancing down, she saw what was written on it: 'Lucenzo Salviati, Banco D'Oro'.

Her mouth shaped into an astonished circle as she slowly studied him again. It was the name of the person she was supposed to meet. A dazzling grin of sheer relief spread over her face.

'This is crazy! I've just realised who you are!' she beamed, warmth flooding her voice.

His body stilled like the calm before the storm. 'You have?' he asked warily.

She nodded in delight, everything forgotten other than the fact that she'd have help with her bags and a companion to talk to. 'You're a bank clerk!' she said triumphantly.

He scowled. 'Banker,' he grated tightly through his teeth.

'Oh. My apologies,' she grinned, aware that she'd wounded his massive ego. 'Banker, bank clerk, it makes no difference to me. You'll be glad to hear, Mr Lucenzo Salviati, that your journey wasn't wasted after all!'

The scowl deepened. '*Luchenzo*,' he corrected stiffly. 'How is that?'

'Because,' she said happily, 'I'm Meredith Williams.'

'Meredith. . .!' Lucenzo's mouth clamped shut, any trace of courtesy gone. He seemed to half choke on her name. Meredith's offered hand of greeting dropped limply to her side in bewilderment. Anger was rippling through him so fiercely that his whole body seemed to be shivering uncontrollably. '*Impossible*!' he snarled.

'No, it isn't!' she cried, disconcerted. 'Why should it be impossible?'

'Because Meredith Williams happens to be *male*,' he said flatly. 'I know that for a fact——'.

'Well, this Meredith happens to be female, all the bits between the woolly hat and brown brogues,' she said wrily. 'I know that for a——'

'Don't mess around with me!' he interrupted with the savage snarl of an angry lion, making Meredith take a step back in astonishment. 'Who the hell are you?' he demanded grimly.

'I told you. Meredith. I'm the person you've come to meet,' she said doggedly, puzzled by Lucenzo's tight fury. 'Ada Williams is my grandmother.'

He looked stunned. 'I don't believe it,' Lucenzo muttered in an ominously quiet voice. 'A *woman*?' He swore long and soft beneath his breath. 'The vindictive. . .' He bit off whatever he was going to say and inhaled deeply, smoothing his face into a blank expression so that only the hot glitter in his eyes betrayed his anger. 'You have brothers?' he snapped out suddenly.

Meredith tried to gather her confused thoughts together. She had no idea why Lucenzo should be remotely interested, or why he was waiting in such a fever of anticipation for her answer.

'I'm an only child. There's only me——'

'*Gesù*!' He muttered something and then his tensed muscles relaxed. 'You're bad enough,' he said contemptuously.

Suddenly the penny dropped, and Meredith knew why he'd been prowling about the airport like an angry lion. It wasn't just the interminable waiting, the lateness of the hour, the cold boredom he must have suffered.

It was worse than that. He knew all about the blackmail.

She felt her eyes close, as if to block out everything: the embarrassment, the shock, the deep sense of shame. No wonder he looked as if he wanted to wring her neck. She groaned. All that bottled-up vitriol for the man he'd been waiting for had actually been for *her*.

'This is terrible,' she said, upset. 'You—you realise I'm here because of the—the blackmail?' she croaked, barely managing to say the word.

A cynical eyebrow shot up. 'Well, you don't believe in hiding your intentions, do you?' he said tightly.

She flushed at the implied insult. 'What do you mean?' she cried indignantly. 'Are you suggesting that I've come to——?'

'Continue the extortion your grandmother began?' finished Lucenzo, speaking each word slowly and clearly, to produce the maximum of contempt. 'Yes,' he drawled. 'I am suggesting that. Why else would you bother to come halfway across Europe during Arctic weather conditions?'

'Oh, how *dare* you?' she breathed, aghast. 'Your role is to meet me, not to pass judgement—which you're ill-qualified to make. This matter is between me and Corosini.'

'No. It's between you and me,' he said quietly, his eyes holding her startled gaze with a compelling force.

'I don't deal with middle-men.' She was aware that he'd rocked with the insult, but was too furious and shaken to care. 'I told you in my letter last week that I wanted you to arrange for me to meet him. Tomorrow. Until then, let me pass. I can make my own way to my digs,' she said with great dignity.

Meredith was determined to show him that she could do without arrogant bankers who'd heard half a story and jumped to the wrong conclusions. Whirling like a miniature tornado past Lucenzo's menacing bulk, she pesuaded her legs to stop wobbling by sheer force of will and strode angrily over the deep snow to the nearest bus stop.

'Come here!' he ordered. She ignored him. 'You're being stupid!' he barked irritably.

Meredith bristled at his rudeness and whirled around, hot with temper. 'I am not! You are! People who make snap judgements based on hearsay and flimsy evidence are stupid!' she cried, her small figure quivering with outrage. 'You and Corosini are wrong all down the line. About Gran, about me, and even my sex.' She tossed her head. 'Fancy not even considering the idea that Meredith might be a woman's name!'

'It was your——' He cut off his own words abruptly and stared at her woodenly as if frustrated because she was right.

'Nothing in my letter suggested I was a man. That's one mistake you made. Why don't you admit you might have made others?'

Turning her back defiantly on him, she peered at the timetable, wondering despairingly if she'd ever decipher it before she froze where she stood. There was the crunch of his feet rapidly moving away over the snow and she felt her tense muscles relax. Lucenzo was going. A few moments later, however, a taxi drew up to the kerb and he thrust his golden head out of the window. She groaned silently.

'Get in,' he ordered arrogantly.

'What are you, royalty?' she demanded. His nostrils flared dangerously but she stood her ground. 'I'm not travelling with someone who thinks I'm here intent on blackmail. I'll go it alone.' She drew herself up to her full height. 'But just you wait, Lucenzo Salviati! You'll wish you never——'

The door flew open and Lucenzo exploded out of the cab like a flying demon, catching her arms in a fierce grip, his face distorted with anger. Meredith squealed in alarm as he jerked her roughly towards him.

'Don't you *ever* threaten me,' he whispered, his breath clouding the cold air between them and freezing on her parted lips. 'And, for your information, I've *long* wished that I'd never heard of you—or your wretched grandmother. But you'll get in that darn cab and stop giving me any more hassle, even if I have to throw you in bodily like the little baggage you are. I mean it. So decide whether you get in under your own steam, or with my assistance.'

His vehemence shook her. But she was in the right and so she held her body erect, her tiny, heart-shaped face raised to his in haughty indifference however close to angry tears she might be.

'You think I'm the granddaughter of a criminal——'

'I don't *think*,' he said scornfully. 'I know you are. You've got ten seconds.'

The hard eyes bored into hers mercilessly. She began to tremble, quite appalled by the situation. It was unbelievable that anyone could condemn her like this without good reason.

'You're wrong. I've always been totally honest,' she cried shakily. 'My parents brought me up to——'

'Lie, cheat, steal. Five. . .four. . .'

'Oh!' She wriggled fruitlessly in his ruthless grasp. 'Let me go,' she grated, 'or I'll——'

'You'll what?' rasped Lucenzo, his fingers biting into her arms. 'Don't be ridiculous.' He looked at the stubborn set of her mouth and muttered something— obviously rude—in Italian. 'Don't you know that there isn't a bus till dawn?' he rasped.

'Dawn?' she cried in dismay, all the stuffing knocked out of her.

He took advantage of her despair. Without another word, he picked up her bags and disdainfully threw them into the boot. Miserably she allowed him to settle her in the taxi. She stole an anxious look at him and withered from the frosty blast of his basilisk stare.

'Thank you,' she muttered with chilling politeness.

'Don't. I'd hate you to imagine that I'm doing this out of the goodness of my heart,' he said through clenched teeth. 'We happen to be staying in the same place, and I'm damned if I'm keeping awake waiting for you to turn up. I've had precious little sleep over the last two days because of your delayed flight, and I'm exhausted. That's why you're getting a lift and for no other reason. Understand?'

'Perfectly,' she said stiffly, hoping she sounded unaffected by his undisguised loathing. 'But I will keep my independence. I insist on paying half the fare.'

He shot her a surprised look and shrugged. 'All right. Why should I beggar myself for you?'

She blanched, hardly hearing his barked order at the driver. The cab drove slowly away through the bleak night while Meredith sat without moving, painfully remembering where she'd heard that phrase before: 'Beggar myself'.

It had been nearly a year ago, when the postman had delivered a letter postmarked Venice to the little cottage in Wales she had shared with her grandmother. Gran had read the letter, given an anguished cry and collapsed. Meredith felt the memory freeze her bones, remembering how she'd comforted her paralysed grandmother during the long wait for the ambulance, knowing this was her third heart attack.

Only later did she read the letter. It was from a man called Corosini, demanding the return of a key and threatening to expose her grandmother as a blackmailer. The letter had ended, 'I beggar myself for years because of you. Not any more.'

Even now, recalling it all, a sick feeling churned inside her stomach. The accusation was a crazy mistake. She would have written to the man to protest, but there had been no address, and only when she had power of attorney did she find any link with Venice—the Banco D'Oro.

And now she was face to face with a man who really believed her grandmother was guilty. She took a deep breath for courage. 'What's the connection between you and Corosini?' she ventured quietly.

The dark eyes slanted in her direction briefly and then looked away. 'He has accounts at the bank.'

'I see.' Despite the thudding of her heart, she tried to calm herself and be rational. 'It's natural that you should be on his side, if he's your client. I can understand your attitude to me,' she said evenly.

'How generous of you,' he drawled with heavy sarcasm. 'First you try to disarm me by offering to pay half the fare and now you're telling me I'm allowed to despise a criminal.'

'Criminal!' She winced and lifted enormous, misted blue eyes to his. 'No, no. . . Give me a chance to explain,' she began shakily.

'I'll give you the same chance I'd give a hungry vixen in a rabbit cage,' he growled. 'Don't try soft-soaping me. I'm immune to sweetness and light.'

'Oh, for heaven's sake! Are you condemning me outright?' she snapped with some asperity. A small sigh of expasperation floated from her lips, drawing his frowning attention to them.

'Yes, I am.' He stretched out his hands and insolently took her face in them, studying her with unusual care. He began with her eyes, capturing and holding her with a laser-like stare that probed deep into her brain. And then he concentrated on her mouth, his head angling to one side as if contemplating a take-over bid.

She felt an overwhelming urge to lick her lips and fought it for a while till her treacherous tongue simply shot out—only to be retracted slowly, under Lucenzo's predatory eyes. Meredith swallowed, not knowing why her skin was tingling as if it had been electrified.

'What are you looking for?' she asked huskily.

'Innocence.'

'And?'

There had been an unnerving change in the closed atmosphere of the cab. She was conscious of his deeply sensual masculinity, and for the first time in her life recognised the electrically charged power of a virile male. Bewildered, she shrank back into the corner of the cab and his hands slid away to undo the buttons of his coat, revealing an expensive and elegant black pin-striped suit.

'I'm considering the evidence carefully,' he murmured.

'You don't have all the evidence,' she said slowly.

He loosened his gold tie and then the pale cream collar of his shirt in a gesture so filled with sexual imagery that she found a disturbing warmth flowing through her insides. His deliberate action caused her to wonder nervously what his intentions were. Then she smiled wryly to herself, her humour mercifully returning, for he was giving her shapeless, huddled outline a sourly critical appraisal. This was no farmer's son, she conceded, eager to court the only eligible female within twenty miles!

'You don't look *anything* like the man I was expecting,' he muttered disparagingly.

'Thank you,' she said drily, recovering a little more of her composure. 'I think I'm flattered. Your fevered imagination must have turned Meredith Williams into a cross between a gangland mobster and Satan.' She smiled faintly, deciding to disconcert him with humour. 'Instead of which you've ended up with a half-grown female in a hat like a tea-cosy. I hope you're not disappointed?'

He didn't answer, but this time his lips quirked up as if he was secretly amused by something, and she hoped it was her bravely joking manner. Maybe she could win him over. His next words dashed her hopes.

'Disappointed? Yes, I am. I'd prefer you to be in that snowdrift,' he said in biting tones.

'That's not very nice!' she cried, pink with indignation.

'Neither's blackmail,' he growled.

'I agree,' she retorted grimly. 'And we're going to clear up this misunderstanding, so tell me what you *think* you know about me.'

The blue of her eyes became dark, haunted hollows in her pale face. There were storms raging beneath that rigid male body, and they might break around her head. Small signs betrayed the existence of a dangerously controlled fury: the stiffness of his face, the white line around his lips, the clenched muscles of his thighs. But, whatever the risk, she'd much rather they brought things out into the open.

'I know everything,' he said with a brutal roughness in his voice. 'I'm the one who received your letter to the bank, querying the monthly credits to your grandmother's account.'

'Yes—I wondered,' she said falteringly, 'if there might be a connection between the payments and Corosini's accusation. You never answered my letter,' she added resentfully.

'It was none of your business,' he snapped.

'It certainly was! I said I had power of attorney to deal with Gran's affairs,' answered Meredith defensively.

'But not why.'

'She'd had a heart attack and had been totally paralysed.'

'No. . .*speech*?' he queried, his body as taut as a bowstring.

Meredith barely registered his reaction. 'Poor darling,' she whispered. 'Gran couldn't even write messages to say what she wanted. She tried to, desperately——'

'I bet,' Lucenzo muttered softly.

'You callous devil!' she cried, horrified by his lack of pity. 'I know she'd had two bad attacks before, but I blame Corosini's groundless threats for the last. If I ever had cause to hate anyone, it would be him, and I'm going to tell him so, when I meet him.' Lucenzo's dark eyes flickered in warning but Meredith was determined not to be intimidated. 'Blackmail indeed! How would you like to be an innocent old woman quietly doing your knitting, and then get a letter like that out of the blue?'

'Innocent, hell!'

Meredith wriggled to the edge of the seat, oblivious of anything but the need to put this man straight about her very proper, homely grandmother. 'This is ludicrous!' she exploded. 'How could a scrap of a woman who'd never left the country get mixed up with some crazy Venetian? She didn't even *like* foreigners! She was Welsh to her fingertips. She was suspicious of the *English* as a race, let alone the Italians.'

'You defend her valiantly,' he conceded. 'If unwisely. I could almost admire you for your loyalty.'

'I'd defend any member of my family whose integrity was challenged,' she said passionately. 'Wouldn't you?'

The jaw tightened till it looked as if it had been carved from golden marble. 'I would. I do. My family is my life,' he muttered. His eyes glowed with an extraordinary fervour. 'I would destroy anyone who threatens them.'

'I'm glad you feel that way——' she began huskily, hoping to build on mutual ground.

'Then you're unwise to be glad. Because what I feel puts you in a dangerous position,' he said with silky menace. His eyes mocked her puzzled frown. 'Don't try to work it out. Tell me, why wait so long before coming here?' Languidly he brushed one of his blond hairs from her knee. His hand suddenly closed like a vice, making her jerk sharply. 'Did it take you all that time to invent this story and to select your wardrobe from the charity shops?' he asked with sinister softness.

'You monster! How dare you make fun of my clothes?' she cried. 'I can't help having to make do. And as for the delay in writing, don't you have any idea how time-consuming it is, looking after someone who's been paralysed by a stroke?' She lifted her head defiantly, wanting to spare him nothing and to make him feel an absolute heel. 'I had no time to think,' she said, grinding the words out, 'until the funeral was over.'

If she'd expected signs of embarrassment or even an apology, it was obvious that she'd miscalculated. The hand on her knee withdrew and Lucenzo's body relaxed.

His breath hissed out slowly. 'So she's dead.' He thought for a moment, the silence lengthening. Meredith stared blindly into the darkness, wishing the nerve-jangling journey would end. 'The guilt finally got to her.'

'I've never heard anything so vicious!' she gasped, white-lipped, tears springing hotly to her eyes.

'It's true,' he snapped. 'She'd been taking hush-money for the last ten years.'

'Ten years?' she cried, horrified.

'Hadn't you checked through the old bank statements?' he asked tightly. His black eyes turned as cold as stone. 'Granny's little extortion racket must have built up a small fortune for you.'

She flushed and tried not to let him rile her. 'I'm aware *now* that Gran had a lot of money. It was an incredible shock when I saw how much.'

'I'm sure it was,' mocked Lucenzo.

And then Meredith made an unnerving connection, her eyes widening in alarm. It was ten years ago when her parents had died, in a train crash. And apparently the payments had begun then. A chill ran through her. What was the meaning of that? Compensation? Had her grandmother knowingly taken the money—or. . . maybe demanded it? She bit her lip, trying to shut out the doubt that was creeping through her mind like a seeping disease. Her grandmother also had a very strong sense of natural justice. It would be just like her to expect some recompense for whoever caused the crash. That could have been Corosini.

'I have to trace your client,' Meredith breathed.

Lucenzo's lips curled. 'Of course,' he mocked. 'Your little nest-egg isn't enough for you, is it? You've found the pot of gold, and your greedy little fingers want to scrape it out——'

'No!' she denied vehemently.

'Don't interrupt!' he snapped. 'I'm not used to backchat or defiance! And if you've got any sense at all, you won't underestimate me. Venetians know all about intrigue. Working out what you're up to is child's play.'

'So play ball and tell me my plans, then,' she said resentfully.

'I told you. To carry on the family tradition and blackmail Corosini.'

Meredith's cheekbones stood out raw in her pale face. 'How dare you give your own twisted interpretation of my motives?' she whispered, unbearably distressed by the unfair, vile accusation. She winced as her chin was caught between cruel fingers and tilted up so that her frightened eyes were forced to look into his.

'Stop this charade!' he spat. 'I've warned you already; don't play the sweet innocent with me. I despise your grandmother for what she did—for what she's put Corosini through. And I don't believe for one moment that you could have been ignorant of the fact that she was wealthy. What was she doing, for God's sake?' he scorned. 'Living on bread and jam?'

'Virtually!' she cried, goaded intolerably by his mockery. 'We never had much money! We lived in a rented cottage in a remote Welsh valley with no luxuries. And life was even tougher when I had to give up my job to care for Gran——'

'Oh, come, now,' he said with an unpleasant silkiness. 'You can't expect me to believe this sob story!'

'It's not "sob",' she said proudly. 'I'm not asking for pity. I'm merely explaining——'

'But I know perfectly well that your welfare services would have put her into a home, if she was as poor as you claim——'

'I wouldn't *dream* of letting strangers look after my own grandmother!' she cried indignantly.

'Oh, the loyal and dedicated granddaughter!' He regarded her with total disbelief. 'One would almost imagine,' he said in a low murmur, 'that you had greasepaint in your veins, with such a consistent, quality performance.'

Meredith caught a sinister undertone in his words, and looked at him sharply. 'What do you know about my family?' she demanded.

Perhaps he was aware that her mother had been an actress and he was taunting her, she thought in panic, her pulse-rate increasing dramatically. If so, how did he know? No, she said firmly to herself. He couldn't know—because there wasn't a connection with Corosini. No, *no*!

A nerve jiggled at the corner of Meredith's mouth because she was beginning to piece small bits of information together and was coming up with a heap of worries. Her father had taken her mother's maiden name when they married. He'd said it was a surrender to the inevitable because her actress-mother was the famous one and he kept getting called Mr Williams anyway. Had there been another reason? Her hands trembled.

'Your grandmother had enough money to *buy* a home if she'd wanted to,' Lucenzo observed in a soft growl.

'But I didn't know that!' she cried in frustration. 'Not until I took control of her affairs—and, in any case, I would still have looked after her——'

The fingers tightened and every word he spoke was slow, deliberate and flung at her with malevolent force through his clenched teeth. 'Very convincing. Applause, applause! Pity about the tiny audience for your heart-rending portrayal of genteel poverty and devotion. But then, you're born to it, aren't you?'

'Born. . .? I don't know what you mean!' she whispered hoarsely, searching his frozen face for clues to the mystery.

'No?' His face moved closer, filling her vision.

'Think about it. You don't know much about Venetians, do you?'

'I'm not sure I want to,' she defied bravely.

His lashes flickered in contempt. 'If you did, you'd never try to pull the wool. . .' he reached up and tugged down her hat further over her forehead '. . .over my eyes,' he breathed. She trembled, the apparently playful gesture making her intensely conscious of the superior strength in those broad shoulders and the hunky chest. He treated her to a malicious smile. 'You're wise to be frightened. You should be, if you've been party to extortion. My God! While you've been living it up in the lap of luxury——'

'No, I haven't!' she denied weakly, almost reaching breaking-point. 'I told you. . .' But his blazing black eyes paralysed her, and she knew now how her grandmother had felt, wanting to speak and yet being unable to. Lucenzo's face became misty as the tears formed in her eyes and rolled silently down her cheeks.

'You can turn those off,' he rasped, sounding totally unmoved. 'Life has hardened me beyond pity. I sacrificed all pleasure when I was a child, to work and study twenty hours a day to support my family—while you, damn you to hell, lived like a parasite off Corosini money! *Tainted* money!'

'Oh, please!' she whispered, horrified. 'Don't think this of me——'

'*Basta*! Enough!' His lip curled in scorn. 'It's a waste of your time begging for any compassion from me. I have none. I feel nothing for you. Greed and hypocrisy deserve to be punished.' She quailed under his searing glance over her body. 'I object to the way you've dressed like someone from the pages of a Dickensian workhouse and turned up with your belongings in carrier bags as if you're on your way to the laundromat.'

'My suitcase——'

'Yes, yes, I know the story. It "broke". You insult my intelligence with your crude methods! If that was your misguided attempt to make an appealing, heart-rending entrance into my life, you've failed. I know what you want, and as sure as hell,' he said savagely, his merciless hands holding her a prisoner, 'I'll stop you from getting it.'

CHAPTER TWO

MEREDITH clung to the edge of the seat, terrified by the suppressed violence in every inch of Lucenzo's body. He looked ready to throw her out of the moving taxi. Calm him, she thought.

'All I want is to clear my name,' she told him quietly. 'And to clear up the mistake. I want to persuade Corosini to stop these payments——'

'*Gesù*! You are making me very, very angry,' he broke in softly. She met his blazing eyes and flinched, wishing he'd yell. This daunting, deliberate control of his voice and of his emotions was doubly unnerving. 'You're overplaying the role you've written for yourself.'

'Not if I and my grandmother have been innocent of blackmail!' she said, weariness washing over her. This man was as hard as iron. 'I swear, I'm totally mystified, Lucenzo. Isn't it possible that there's been an error— a computer error, perhaps? Could Corosini have paid money to the wrong person? Neither Gran nor my parents have ever been in Italy. I know that, because Gran said so once, when we were going through an atlas together. They certainly never mentioned Venice——'

'Didn't they?' He studied her minutely for a long time until she felt his eyes had bored into her very skull.

'I'm not a liar,' she said quietly. 'How can I convince you? Can't you give me the benefit of the doubt? There's been a mix-up of account numbers or something.' Her voice began to shake. 'Stop the payments, I beg you!'

'Don't overdo this act,' he drawled. 'I might take you at your word——'

'I wish you would. It's what I want,' she mumbled in exhaustion.

'An error,' he said slowly, eyeing her trembling hands as they twisted on her lap. 'We could agree on that.' He hesitated. 'I could arrange to stop the payments,' he said cautiously.

She sensed an excitement in him and wondered why, but she was too tired to think at the moment. 'Look, if you knew my gran, you'd know why I'm so certain about this,' she said earnestly, knowing this was her chance to persuade him. 'She was as straight as a die and a pillar of the community. I can get people to write to you saying so. The minister, for instance. You'd believe a man of God, wouldn't you?'

'Of course.'

Meredith's forehead cleared, sensing that he was really listening at last. 'My grandmother went to chapel twice on Sunday, paid a tenth of her pension to charity and read the Bible every day. She never did a wrong thing in her life. She was incredibly strict and had terribly high moral standards, believing everyone was accountable in the end for whatever they did. Does that sound like a blackmailer?'

'Not a lot,' he conceded. 'But if what you say is true, then at the very least she was guilty of accepting money under false pretences. She should have queried the fact that her bank balance was looking like the population figure for Naples.'

Meredith bit her lip. 'I couldn't work that out either,' she admitted unhappily. 'Perhaps that's what she was trying to explain, after she'd had her stroke.'

'Oh, I'm sure she was,' he said scathingly. 'It must have been a shock, realising that she too was accountable for what she'd done.'

'You swine!' gasped Meredith. He shrugged. She forced herself to keep on an even keel. 'Gran wasn't interested in banks, and didn't understand accounts. She kept her cash in a shoebox under the bed. There haven't been any withdrawals,' she added anxiously. 'I can show you the statements later.'

'No withdrawals?' A faint frown of doubt brought Lucenzo's brows together. 'But. . .' He saw her curious eyes on him and appeared to change tack. 'Perhaps she was saving it for you.'

'Me? I don't. . .' Her voice trailed away and her blue eyes widened.

'Yes?' prompted Lucenzo silkily.

She bit her lip. 'She—she said once that she'd see I was all right,' said Meredith, reluctantly honest.

'Now we're getting there,' he said in sardonic approval. 'One thing. . . If you're as poor as you claim and the money is untouched, who paid for your flight?'

'That came out of my savings,' she answered simply. 'Every penny I had in the world.' She swallowed back the lump in her throat.

He snorted in disbelief. 'You're telling me that you spent every penny of your personal money to come over here and clear your late grandmother's name?'

'Yes! Now you see how important it is to me!' she cried passionately.

'You could have taken the money and kept quiet,' he said abruptly.

'Of course I couldn't!' she said with irritation. 'I've hardly been able to sleep because of all this worry. I had to come, however much I hated the idea. It's not been much fun so far,' she said mournfully.

'Extortion never is. Meredith, you're either very clever, or unbelievably naïve. I can't decide. However, if none of the money has been touched. . .' He shrugged, an enigmatic smile on his face. 'I'm half inclined to believe you.'

'Oh, Lucenzo, thank you!' she cried fervently, grasping his arm in gratitude.

His muscles tensed. 'Please don't touch me,' he said tightly. Her fingers withdrew from the soft cloth and her cheeks went rose-pink with humiliation. 'I didn't say I *did* believe you. I'm merely reserving judgement.

Though I have a suggestion that would solve this delicate situation for all of us.'

'Tell me,' she urged, a little surprised at his sudden capitulation. 'Anything.'

'Good,' he purred. 'Go home on the first flight out of here. I'll speak to Corosini, explain the mistake and speak up on your behalf. I'm sure he'll be only too glad to cancel the payments, and nothing more will be said.' His eyes slid to hers. 'If you like, I'll persuade him to let you keep the money that's already been paid over——'

'Absolutely not!' she said, suspicious of his motives. 'I don't let someone else do my dirty work for me. For my own peace of mind, I have to see this man face to face. I want us both to part as friends. And I keep telling you, I don't want the wretched money,' she said vehemently. 'How can I keep it if it's not mine?'

He looked at her askance. And then smiled a slow, knowing smile. 'You went a little bit too far there, Meredith,' he said quietly. 'So you'll waive all rights to the money and—despite the fact that you claim Corosini hastened your grandmother's death—you want to meet him so you can say hello? And "part as friends"?'

'Yes,' she said simply, wondering why he was so incredulous. 'What's wrong with that? You'll help, won't you?'

He gave a short, humourless laugh. 'Like hell I will, you little witch! You must think I've just crawled out of my crib!' His cold black eyes met Meredith's, and she stared at him in dismay. 'I've been around too long to fall for tricks like that. You've got an ulterior motive for seeing Corosini.'

'No, I haven't!' she yelled, her patience snapping. 'It's just that I can't stand the slur on my grand-mother's memory. I have to set the record straight. Self-respect means more to me than mere money——'

'*Mere* money? My dear girl, it's a small fortune! No

one in her right mind would turn her back on that! If you think I'd believe such crazy behaviour, you've miscalculated my knowledge of human nature.' His hand mockingly stroked her indignant face, the light touch sending shivers of danger down her spine. 'What a sweet thing you pretend to be! *Che bella honesta! Mille complimente, signorina!*'

Meredith fumed at his liquefying eyes and the contemptuous curl of his sculpted mouth. He was so utterly convinced of his own rightness that there was no way she could persuade him of her innocence at this moment. But she would, she thought grimly. And she'd extract a very, very humble apology when she did. He'd eat ashes!

'All right, that's it,' she snapped, uneasy at the triumphant expression in his molten black eyes.

'You give in?' he murmured, his lips tantalisingly close to her face.

'No!' she cried shakily. 'You won't listen, you won't believe me and you're too darned sure of yourself to consider you might be wrong. So I'm staying in Venice to find out for myself what's been going on.'

Lucenzo's feelings were totally masked. 'Venice is very good at keeping its secrets,' he murmured with a maddeningly superior smile.

'You don't give an inch, do you?' she said wearily.

'No,' he agreed, his glittering black eyes holding hers with their remorseless stare. 'Not an inch. If you insist on staying, I warn you, you'll get no help from me. You might as well go home now.' His voice softened to a menacing growl. 'I suggest you would be sensible to do so. Otherwise you'll get involved in a situation you'll wish you'd never walked into.'

'I don't run away from my responsibilities,' she said with a confidence she didn't feel.

'Then it won't be long before you wish you had,' he answered, turning his back on her.

* * *

It was a long drive from the airport, made tedious by the unnatural, tense silence in the cab. Meredith felt as if her nerves were strung on a line. Because of Lucenzo's hostility and suspicious nature it might be very difficult fishing out the truth. But she *had* to see Corosini. The man was either mad or deluded.

And she wouldn't let Lucenzo crush her. She recalled that he'd spoken with passion about his family. . . If he was devoted to his wife and children then he must have a soft heart beneath that refrigerated exterior. She must persevere with him.

At last Lucenzo buttoned his coat, and she pulled on her woollen gloves just as the taxi came to a halt. '*Allora*. The Piazzale Roma.' He indicated the huge, snow-swept square. 'It's as far as we can go. Cars aren't allowed beyond this point.' He extracted a beautiful leather wallet from his pocket and looked at her in challenge. 'Now pay your dues.'

Meredith eased her cramped limbs from the taxi. 'How much is it?' she asked, anxiously leafing through the foreign currency in her purse.

'Is that all you have?' he asked, frowning.

'Yes,' she said, adding proudly, 'but I can cash some more tomorrow.'

His long, slender fingers extracted some notes—most of them, she was appalled to see. 'That's fine, then,' he said curtly. Seeing her startled face, he grunted. 'Not used to paying your way?' he suggested.

The corners of her mouth lifted ruefully. 'Wrong. I'm just not used to extravagance. But I always go Dutch. My boyfriends are penniless to a man.' She saw his baffled expression and smiled faintly. 'I don't choose my friends for the size of their wallets, you know.'

'Really.' By his expression, it was clear that he thought she was lying. 'The water-taxis are over there,' he said evenly.

'And they're expensive, I'm sure. Walking is cheaper,' she said, a little irritated that he hadn't got the message. 'Maybe a banker can afford them, but I bet I can't.'

'I'm tempted to let you struggle through Venice on your own, after that contrived mini-lecture on working-class thrift,' he drawled.

'Heaven give me strength!' she seethed, turning away.

'Come back! I'll pay this time, if that's your objection,' he said. His eyes grew hard and calculating. 'You won't mind sweeping about Venice on my money, will you?'

'Yes. I would. Do what you please. I couldn't accept any favours from you or waste money unnecessarily. I'm walking.' She pulled her map of Venice from her coat pocket, a determined expression on her face.

'A woman, stopping me from spending money?' he exclaimed in surprise. 'I don't know whether you're being considerate, crafty, or just plain calculating.'

'Try careful.' Meredith was surprised he always had to look for a hidden motive. She sighed. Venetians didn't appear to be straightforward at all.

'So you walk?' He raised his eyebrows at her nod, as if the idea was astounding, then picked up her bags in resignation while the taxi driver stared at him open-mouthed. Lucenzo muttered something to the man, who grinned understandingly.

'Thank you,' she said quietly, deciding not to protest at his reluctant gesture of chivalry.

'Both of us are going to regret this,' Lucenzo muttered, as they began to cross the bleak, unprepossessing square.

She didn't, at first, because she was fascinated. Venice was obviously a city to be seen on foot or, better still, she thought dreamily, by slow gondola, because everything was on the human scale without a city block in sight. They trudged across the crunching snow over tiny, hump-backed bridges which spanned the silent black canals and wound their way through a labyrinth of deserted streets—some hardly wider than Lucenzo's broad shoulders.

Meredith glanced up uncertainly at the four-storey buildings soaring up forbiddingly on either side of the alley where they were walking. To her it seemed that they were closing in on her, and she looked ahead nervously, seeing that Lucenzo's rapid stride had taken him out of sight. Alone in the hushed half-darkness, she feared he was trying to lose her, to teach her a lesson. All she could hear was the sound of his footsteps on the fresh snow and the swish and bump of her bags as they scraped the alley walls.

'Lucenzo!' she called quaveringly. 'Where are you?'

'*Qui. A destra*. On the right. Keep up,' he called back irritably, his voice echoing in the silence.

She dashed around the corner, glad to see his dark bulk again. For the moment, he represented security to her. 'It's a long way,' she complained when she joined him, pushing down her brief panic, quite embarrassed by her own wild fears.

'You're the one who wanted to walk,' he reminded her shortly.

'I know,' she agreed with a sigh. 'But I'd forgotten how tired I was. You see, I didn't have any cash to spare last night for a hotel at Heathrow when the plane was delayed, so I spent the night on the airport floor——'

'Who writes this stuff for you?' he complained. 'You'd be a better actress with better lines.'

'I'm not an actress,' she said stubbornly, alerted again by his uncanny reference to her mother's profession. Or perhaps she was being paranoid, and it was chance.

'Just ease up on the drama. I'm not interested. If you didn't like what was happening, you should have taken a curtain call and gone home,' he said coldly, totally without pity.

'Gone home?' she cried in astonishment. 'I don't give up. I'm the ultimate in stubborn.'

The suspicion of a frown crossed his imperturbable face. 'Well, isn't that a coincidence?' he said with soft menace. 'So am I. But you're on my territory now. I have the advantage, Meredith, and I intend to use it against you.'

Finding his animosity wearing, she stared at him wide-eyed, the snow drifting down on to her upturned face. 'I don't know why you don't push me in a canal,' she said sulkily, her mouth pouting.

His finger tested its softness. Startled, her lips parted, and for a moment she tasted the warm firmness of his flesh before she hastily closed her mouth, trapping his finger. Slowly, with a lazy glance, he removed it, leaving her feeling quite weak.

'Neither do I,' he rasped huskily. 'Unless, of course,' he said with a faintly sinister smile, 'I'm saving you for something else.'

Meredith lowered her head to hide the fact that she was having to swallow away the dryness in her throat. To counteract the effect of Lucenzo's sensuality, she tucked her woolly scarf more firmly around her neck then dragged her pom-pom hat further over her reddening ears.

He'd already left her, however, slipping into a tunnel leading right beneath a crumbling building. Hesitantly she followed, her heart in her mouth, creeping nervously through the dark, dank walkway. When she emerged, she found herself in a small square beside a canal so wide that she immediately realised it must be the Grand Canal itself. She stopped, entranced.

'Oh, I've never, ever seen anything so beautiful,' she said inadequately, her fatigue forgotten.

Lucenzo's flowing, feral stride along the quayside faltered. He turned, his blond hair gleaming a liquid gold beneath an ancient wall-lamp. 'Of course you haven't. This is Venice,' he said with great arrogance, his bearing as autocratic as a prince's.

'If only I could see it as a tourist one day,' she said

wistfully. 'But I won't have the time or the opportunity again.'

Virgin snow lay heaped on royal-blue tarpaulins which covered glistening black gondolas riding gently on the dark, silky water. Even the boldly striped mooring posts were topped with a dollop of white, rather like gaudy Cornetto ice-creams. The silence was total. Breathless with excitement, Meredith scanned the stretch of stunning palaces which lined the canal, feeling a sense of awe. They looked as if they'd come out of a medieval illustration.

'What are you doing?' asked Lucenzo impatiently, obviously wanting to hurry on. 'Hoping some prince will come out and invite you in?'

She grinned. 'Of course not! No, I was just rubber-necking. Wondering about the palaces, and dreaming.' She smiled pensively. 'Fancy living in a palace!'

'Envious?' he asked, sounding interested.

'Of the Venetian nobility?' She laughed. 'I bet they have their problems, like us. Like finding a decent window-cleaner to do all those lattice windows. They must be the very devil.'

He allowed himself a slight smile. 'Yes. They must.' His eyes were thoughtful. 'But think of the compensations in being an aristocrat: power, social position, respect,' he said with quiet passion, speaking half to himself.

Meredith was silent for a moment. Being a banker wasn't enough; Lucenzo obviously coveted the things he'd mentioned. 'I imagine glittering *contessas* drinking cocktails on those romantic terraces,' she said dreamily. 'With lunch beneath the rose pergolas to follow. . . It must be wonderful, watching the world float by while you eat lobster and drink champagne. I wonder what it *is* like, living in a building built five hundred years ago?'

He gave her a sideways look. 'Cold,' he said succinctly. 'Damp.'

Her mouth twitched. 'You're no romantic,' she chided.

'I haven't the time for romance,' he said shortly.

'There speaks a workaholic,' she observed with faint disapproval. 'Banking isn't everything. You should make time for dreams.'

'I have dreams. I *make* them come true.' He stared into the distance where the canal curved sinuously, disappearing out of sight. 'I work till I drop to achieve what I want.'

'I'm ambitious, too,' she said confidingly, thinking of the crèche she wanted to own one day. It had been long planned in her mind. If she were rich, that wouldn't stop her caring for children, but she could charge only a nominal fee to the mothers who badly needed to work. 'The things I could do if only I had oodles of cash,' she added with an intense longing.

'You've got enough, haven't you?' he muttered.

'I haven't,' she said stubbornly.

Lucenzo rolled his eyes to the dark sky flaked with stars and softly falling snow. 'What greed! Take my advice,' he drawled. 'Be satisfied with what you have and invest it well. With care, you can realise all your ambitions without lifting a finger. Of course, I'd expect you to sign an affidavit promising not to extort any more money from Corosini.'

'I can't do that,' she frowned. She wasn't going to keep the money. How could she?

'I see. Thank you for letting me know where you stand,' Lucenzo said quietly.

Meredith smiled absently. 'That's all right. I shall have to keep my eyes open for a millionaire while I'm here,' she joked.

Lucenzo grunted. 'You're obsessed by money, aren't you?'

'It's constantly on my mind,' she agreed solemnly, thinking how hard she had to budget.

'I must warn my wealthy clients,' he said cynically.

She chuckled ruefully. 'Don't bother. They wouldn't

be interested in me. I'm far too unsophisticated for you Venetians.'

'Hmm. So you claim. I'm unconvinced. This is it.' He gestured abruptly to the side of a vast building at one end of the square, lit by flaring torches which guttered and spat in the light snowfall.

'Good grief! Your family live in that?' she asked in amazement. For it had obviously been a palace once, the high Gothic arches of the medieval windows and the carved stone Romeo-and-Juliet balconies giving it a fairy-tale air.

Lucenzo gave a bitter smile. 'The *palazzo* doesn't belong to my family.' He was silent for a moment. 'It's . . .divided into rooms.'

Her imagination conjured up a vision of the young, ambitious Lucenzo, struggling to study for his banking exams and to stay smart amid the chaos caused when a wife and several children lived in a cramped apartment. She gave him a warm, friendly look, touched by the thought of his devotion to them—and brightened at the thought of playing with his children.

'I think you're lucky to live there,' she said, admiring the palace. 'It's such a wonderful position, and it must look quite spectacular from the canal. I wish I could see the front properly. Is it very grand inside?'

'Very. Grand enough to satisfy even you,' he said, mocking her eager, sparkling eyes. 'Don't get ideas. The apartment is exquisite, but small.' He grinned at a secret joke. 'It took a lot of work to turn it into exactly what I wanted.'

He opened a small side-door and walked into a small side-hall. Briefly, as she followed Lucenzo across the marble floor, she caught a glimpse inside a dark, spacious room where she could just make out the shape of elegant furniture and banners hanging from a painted ceiling lit by the light from the hall. But then they began to climb up a narrow, spiral staircase, and she saw no more.

Lucenzo dragged her bags with him and muttered

under his breath about their bulk while Meredith stoically forced her exhausted body after his dark figure, her legs aching with the long climb.

'Home at last,' he said cynically.

In semi-darkness, she waited, hearing the sound of a key grating against metal, and then he fumbled for a moment, muttering to himself in Italian. 'What's wrong?' she frowned.

'Can't find the——Ah. Got it.' Light flooded a large, high-ceilinged room with huge, full-length window shutters.

'This is small?' she cried.

'Compared with—well, yes,' he frowned. 'Welcome to my room.' He gave a mocking bow.

Her eyes dropped from the massive glass chandelier and swept around the apartment. A hasty glance took in the gorgeous antique furniture crammed in as if it had been recently off-loaded by a dealer, the small, pristine cooker and the sink pushed against the soft ochre-washed wall as if it was an after-thought. And the two single sleigh beds, side by side.

No welcoming wife, no laughing toddlers. And, judging by the minimum of personal clutter, no family at all. 'Where—where's my room?' she stammered.

Lucenzo gave a slow smile. 'You're looking at it,' he said in a lazy drawl, easing off his jacket.

Meredith averted her eyes from the breadth of muscular chest sharply defined beneath the crisp linen shirt by the movement. 'You mean we're. . .' her voice went croaky '. . .together? In here?' She registered his sardonic nod with dismay. 'But. . .your family. . .'

'We all thought I was old enough to manage on my own,' he said laconically.

She glared at his ridicule. 'You know perfectly well that I can't stay in here with you,' she mumbled.

'It's all there is.' Lucenzo seemed vastly pleased. He tipped the contents of her bags on to one of the beds. 'Don't tell me you haven't shared a room with a man before?' he murmured.

Two bright spots of colour stood out on Meredith's creamy cheeks. 'No! Of course I haven't!' she cried indignantly.

'Then it's about time you did,' he said, indifferent to her embarrassment. Throwing his jacket on the gold damask counterpane, he smiled at her over his shoulder. 'This is my bed. That's yours.'

She stared at him in horror. 'You can't mean this!' she cried. 'I thought you were married! You gave that impression; that's why I came up here with you——'

'Don't blame me for the way you interpret anything I say,' he said blandly.

'But. . . I wouldn't have dreamed of sharing. . . Lucenzo, are you doing this to make me go home?'

'Now why would I want to do that?' he asked mildly. 'Meredith, I explained. I thought I was meeting a man. It seemed a sensible solution for us to share this room.'

'Why? You loathed the idea of meeting the person who——'

'If I couldn't get rid of him straight away, then I meant to keep an eye on him,' he interrupted grimly.

Her lower lip trembled. She was so very tired, and all she wanted was to sleep and sleep. But not with Lucenzo's cold black eyes finding fault with her every hour of the night. 'Take me to another room,' she demanded miserably. 'You have to!'

'I can't,' he answered smugly, thrusting his hands into his pockets and surveying her small, unhappy figure. 'I told you about the Carnival when I replied to your last letter. I said you were mad to come over at this time. It's a world event. Don't you know that Venice is packed with visitors?'

'I didn't see any,' she frowned.

'In the early hours? In this weather? They're not all mad. But the rooms are taken, I can assure you. Even the pigeons have had to reserve accommodation. I can confirm that there are no spare rooms in the whole of this city.'

'There must be!' she wailed, her eyes darting everywhere in a vain hope that there was somewhere she could go. 'That door. . .where does that lead?'

'It's. . .' For an extraordinary moment, because of the faint frown he gave, Meredith thought he wasn't sure, and then he recovered his poise. 'Find out,' he challenged.

She did. 'A cupboard,' she said in disappointment. 'And that one?'

This time, he appeared to know. 'Bathroom. The floor's marble. Awfully cold,' he told her with malicious pleasure.

She leaned helplessly against the wall. There was less than a yard between the beds. The place was so full of heavy furniture that there was no room to rearrange the beds further apart. She bit her lip. It was far too intimate a situation. With far too masculine a man. Her huge eyes filled with tears of frustration.

'I'll have to go out again and search,' she insisted desperately, wondering where. 'Perhaps somewhere on the mainland. . .'

A faint look of admiration came into his eyes and then his long, cloaking lashes had swept down and she was left staring at his mask-like face again.

'Do you think that several thousand visitors haven't thought of that already? Give in for once. What a tough woman you are! I can see I won't have an easy ride with you.'

'A what?' she cried, aghast.

A heavy sigh of exasperation lifted his big chest, drawing her worried eyes. 'Meredith,' he said, sounding irritable, 'I don't want to stand here discussing this. I want to get some sleep, not indulge in erotic horse-play—after all, you might blackmail me after,' he said cuttingly. 'Besides, I've never been consumed with lust for the caress of a grey woollen glove.'

His insolent mockery made her flush with indignation. And, in an impulsive gesture of totally uncharacteristic vanity, she defiantly yanked open her old coat to reveal her clinging emerald-green sweater and matching stretch cords, and noted the fact that his attention had been arrested by what had lain beneath her outer wrapping. Slowly, with some satisfaction, she peeled off her hand-knitted gloves and dragged off her sensible hat.

Like an imprisoned animal, her vibrant coppery hair bounced out as if alive, tumbling in a glowing red river over her slender shoulders. Truculently she pushed her hands through the glossy waves and then froze, suddenly aware of Lucenzo's prolonged intake of breath.

What had she done? she groaned inwardly. Why had she behaved like a temptress in a fifties movie? She'd never deliberately tried to grab a man's attention before. But, quite inexplicably, she'd hated the thought that Lucenzo found her unappealing. That fact had aroused her enough to make her display her feminine assets to best advantage. She bit her lip in confusion, alarmed at the wash of warmth in her body. Oh, vanity, vanity! she thought, reproaching herself.

Lucenzo had a glint in his eyes which told her she could be in trouble. Her ribcage lifted and her chin tilted up in self-defence to warn him off, but he seemed to interpret that as a provocatively brazen invitation.

'Well,' he drawled. 'This is more like it.' He folded brawny arms across his chest, eyeing her taut, curvy body up and down with a leisured, insolent appraisal. 'The disguise is off. *Bravo*! Pure theatre.'

'No,' she denied.

'Please!' he protested. 'Don't put yourself down. You have a wonderful sense of the dramatic. The butterfly emerges from the chrysalis, the duckling becomes the swan, Cinderella dazzles the prince.' His mouth twisted at some private irony. 'Nicely timed, Meredith. The maximum of surprise and pleasure at the most appropriate moment.' His eyes lanced hers. 'Amazing what's hidden beneath the surface, isn't it? One can never quite believe what one sees. Lovely hair. Get it from your father?'

She blinked. Her highly alerted state of mind told

her there was some purpose behind that question. She was beginning to discover that Lucenzo chose his words carefully and he didn't indulge in idle remarks or mere social chit-chat. But why show interest in the colour of her father's hair? One possibility came to mind. Some imagined connection with Corosini.

'I very much doubt it,' she answered coldly, pleased to disprove whatever theory Lucenzo might be harbouring.

'Don't you know?' he asked, tension in his voice.

She looked at him curiously. 'No. I don't. Father was grey-haired, even when I was tiny.'

'Grey.' His lashes flickered but he continued to probe. 'Surely the photographs of him as a younger man——'

'I don't have any. I shouldn't think he was red-haired, because he tanned easily. Dark, probably, because of his olive skin.'

A nagging little voice reminded her how reticent her father had been about his past, always changing the subject abruptly so that she never learnt a thing about him. It was as if he'd come to her mother like a refugee, because there were no mementoes of his childhood or his youth. She winced. There was nothing to mark his existence. The bonfire had seen to that.

'So your mother's the one with red hair,' said Lucenzo.

'It's called Titian,' she said, pushing her waves back with vigorous sweeps of her hands as if to deny its attraction to men. And this one in particular.

'He would have loved to paint you,' Lucenzo said huskily. 'Titian, that is. Ever been painted, Meredith?'

'Once, with greasepaint.' She saw the querying eyebrow and decided to satisfy his curiosity. The more they talked, the more it might damp down his surprising sexual interest. There was still a rather unnerving gleam in his eyes. She tried not to even consider the soft swell of his expressive mouth, and gabbled on to break the tense atmosphere. 'I took over a part in *A Midsummer Night's Dream*.'

'You *are* an actress!'

She started, remembering his accusations, and went on reluctantly, 'No! I was eleven—and doing my lessons backstage. My mother was the actress, you see.'

He nodded and smiled encouragingly, his eyes as sweet and dark as Turkish coffee. 'How interesting,' he murmured, moving towards her with total self-assurance in every step.

Meredith's mouth felt dry from the waves of sheer sensuality pulsing towards her. Panic galvanised her into action. She pretended to be engrossed in exploring the room, and managed to keep a foot or so away from him as he followed, making her uncomfortably aware of the wall of his body close behind her while she ran her hands over the antique furniture with an assumed interest.

'Lovely chair,' she said blindly, stroking the subtly sensual curves of a fruitwood chair.

'You like to touch, to caress objects. And you like expensive things,' he said softly.

Meredith snatched her hand away hastily. 'I like beautiful things. Did you inherit these?' she asked, dying to find out about his background.

'Tell me about your acting début. How did you get the part?'

'Well, in the play, Puck the fairy is supposed to say he'll put a girdle around the earth in forty minutes——'

'I know the plot,' interrupted Lucenzo drily.

'Oh! You surprise me. Well, Puck broke his leg. Everyone thought there'd be a roar of ribald laughter at that line if Puck happened to be hopping around the stage in plaster at the time.'

Lucenzo burst into laughter himself, and she wished he hadn't, a sharp jolt of awareness rocketing through her body at the dazzling transformation of his face and the deep, warm sound that had travelled through her to her tingling toes. If he ever decided to turn the full wattage of his charm on a woman, she thought, distractedly folding some of her clothes into neat piles, he'd be quite irresistible.

She felt the merest of touches on her hair and then she was being slowly turned around. Her heart pumped like mad, her body still electrified by the devastating appeal of his laughing face. It was unfair, she thought in panic. She wasn't used to such handsome men paying her attention.

Lucenzo's eyes were fiercely alert, his high-peaked mouth fatally dominating Meredith's vision. 'Are you good?' he asked quietly.

'At what?' she husked.

'Let's stick to acting for the moment,' he drawled. 'Had you picked up the skills by watching your mother?'

She attempted to shift her gaze and break away from the invisible hold he had on her. They were only eyes, she told herself sternly. 'Yes, I suppose I had.'

'You enjoyed playing a part,' he murmured.

She forced her voice down an octave. 'Yes, it was fun,' she answered huskily, 'but I never wanted to act for a living——'

'For a hobby, maybe?' he queried.

'No,' she said, wary of his pursuit of the point. 'I never had the time, even if I'd wanted to take it up. I always knew I wanted to work with children, you see.'

'Children! How charming! The perfect choice.'

'I—I don't know what you mean,' she stammered.

'Liar. I hope you're not going to give me as much trouble as Puck gave to the lovers in the play,' Lucenzo murmured, a sliver of steel-tipped menace in his tone.

'Of course not,' she breathed, her eyes huge with apprehension. 'I'm not devious and underhand like him. Besides, he had magic on his side.'

Lucenzo's thick black lashes swept down on to his high cheekbones, and she felt the coolness of his breath on her face. A quiver ran through her which heated as it travelled through her body and which he must have noticed, for he smiled mockingly at her. She felt her breasts rise with her shortened breath, and it seemed as if they were straining to brush his well-developed chest. Her eyes closed briefly in despair. She was an innocent compared with this man, and resented his deliberate use of sex to disconcert her.

'Magic. We all have it, for the right person. That chemical exchange between man and woman, that extraordinary kick in the solar plexus. . .and, deeper still, in places more intimate, more carnal——' As his warm honey voice spread through her, Meredith wondered how on earth he knew what was happening to her. She lifted drowsy blue eyes to his, bemused by the power he seemed to have over her. 'You know,' he was musing throatily, 'I'm very glad you're not a man.' His warm hands moved smoothly over her shoulders and he gave a short laugh. 'You won't ever realise *how* glad.'

'I hope you don't imagine that you can take advantage of me,' she managed, her voice croaking hoarsely.

'I intend to try,' he said drily.

Her lips seemed glued together. With an effort, she made them part, and then her vocal cords let her down by refusing to work. Helplessly she blinked up at him, feeling a slow lethargy creep through her whole body. It must be exhaustion. That would explain the light-headedness, too. She swayed, her lashes dropping over her enormous lagoon-blue eyes.

'Oh, I'm so tired,' she mumbled miserably.

'Nice cue,' he said in a sexy growl, slowly releasing her. 'Time we went to bed, don't you think?' With his gaze locked on hers, he slowly began to undo the buttons of his shirt.

CHAPTER THREE

IT WAS several paralysed seconds before Meredith's befogged brain registered what he was doing, and by then she was staring with darkening eyes at a beautifully toned naked chest. Honey-brown, she thought wildly. Sleek, with skin gleaming like a rich satin——

'Ohhh!' she gasped, coming to her senses.

Reddening with a flush that heated her whole body, she grabbed her wash-bag and night things, and fled for the bathroom, locking the door to the sound of his low, mocking laugh.

'Little tease!' came his cynical voice.

She stood stock-still, panting, listening to the harsh rasp of her own breathing. He would have stripped completely while she watched. Nakedness wouldn't embarrass him—Lucenzo was quite without shame. In the elegant gilt mirror she caught a glimpse of her panic-stricken face, and her eyes flashed like bright, angry sapphires because she had let herself be manipulated like an ignorant country girl. Which she was, of course, she sighed. Her world was opening up with a vengeance.

Her face grew stormy. Lucenzo had been hell-bent on intimidating her from the beginning. He obviously meant to milk the situation for all he was worth. . . Her breathing calmed. Yes, she thought—because he liked power and it amused him to practise dominating people on her. This situation would be one humdinger of a funny story to tell his city friends over a drink or two—and perhaps to boast to Corosini that he'd wrapped her around his little finger with a few husky phrases and a glimpse of his superlative body.

Her chin stuck up into the air. Someone ought to strike a blow for women and show this vain man that he was utterly resistible! She grinned. He'd *die* when he saw her nightdress!

Meredith continued to smile to herself while she washed and changed into her warm, unbelievably prim nightdress and dressing-gown. Passion-killers both, she thought with a mischievous grin. Pity she didn't have curlers or face-ceam. This was no time to look gorgeous. Boldly she opened the door.

His head turned on the pillow towards her when she came in. The impossibly blond hair seemed dishevelled and appealingly boyish, as if he'd been tossing restlessly. For a split second he looked oddly vulnerable, but then he pushed himself up in the bed, her wary eyes lingered on the naked gold of his shoulders, and she quickly changed her mind. He was a dangerous male who was ruthless enough to humiliate and even degrade her if necessary. Even her thick nightdress seemed alarmingly minimal beneath his slow and deliberate contemplation. He had X-ray eyes, she declared in a private panic.

'Where's the frilly nightie?' he drawled.

'The frills fell off,' retorted Meredith cheerfully, willing herself to walk normally across the room and suffer his amused appraisal.

'It's not even low-cut or see-through,' he complained.

'I'd get frostbite in this weather,' she scorned.

'I didn't expect you to carry out your pose as a sweet little innocent *quite* so thoroughly,' he murmured. 'Isn't it time we began the sexy seduction scene? I *am* disappointed.'

'Tough.' Meredith tossed her glorious hair and saw Lucenzo's eyes kindle. She frowned, her heart thumping erratically, and reminded herself not to do that again.

There was a long pause while she cleared the bed of her things, and she was aware of his eyes on her every movement as he checked over the items she'd packed for any signs of decadence. Naturally he found none.

He was very still, as if he was weighing up what she'd said. Then a soft sigh escaped his alarmingly voluptuous lips. Hazily, Meredith tried to recall if they'd always looked so intensely inviting.

'Your nightie has a hole in it,' he murmured.

She clapped her hand over the bit he was peering at. 'Moths.' She prayed that he couldn't see any flesh. A glimpse of ankle might set him off. He didn't need much of an excuse.

'I do believe that's what you always wear to bed,' he said in amazement. He scowled at her from under his brows. 'And. . . I have an alarming feeling that you might actually be a virgin.'

Her eyes widened. 'Of *course* I am!' she cried heatedly, quite aghast that he should think otherwise.

He looked quite nonplussed. 'Good grief!' he groaned. 'Just my luck. Pure as the driven snow. *Madonna*!'

'It's nothing to ridicule,' she said haughtily. 'Where I come from, it's normal. My father would turn in his grave if he knew I'd ever. . .ever. . .'

'Slept with a man? You're going to tonight,' Lucenzo pointed out wryly, his mouth lifting in a fascinating curve.

Meredith dragged her eyes away from it reluctantly. 'Only because I don't have any choice. But I'll be untouched and intact in the morning!' she said, her eyes daring him to say otherwise.

'A virgin,' he marvelled, not contradicting her last remark. And not agreeing either. 'And you, the daughter of an actress!'

'Watch that prejudice!' she said hotly. 'Gran brought Mother up very strictly. Mum was never flighty.'

'Indeed.' He looked baffled by the revelation.

'Indeed,' she echoed. 'My mother was a virgin on her wedding night, and that's what I'm going to be,' she said firmly.

'What fascinating revelations you offer me about

your family,' murmured Lucenzo, still apparently thrown off-balance by what she was saying.

He gave an exaggerated stretch, displaying the powerful biceps and the soft inside skin of his arms. Silk one side, she thought in fascination, steel strength the other. He was a man of contrasts. His ribcage had lifted, expanding his chest, and she saw the dark golden hair running in a faint line down to his waist. It was difficult not looking at him, but she forced herself to show an interest in brushing her hair.

'I was making a point about my morals,' she said primly.

'You've made it,' he said languidly, watching the light turning her waves to a red-gold. 'OK, I won't try to battle my way past all that camouflage for the treasures that lie beneath. There's always tomorrow.'

'T-tomorrow?' she croaked. Her eyes widened, seeing his body through the mirror. Meredith might be a virgin, but she knew when a man was aroused. And beneath that exquisite, soft blue blanket his half-naked body was plainly outlined, inch by virile inch.

'Goodnight.' He rolled over, and she was left staring at the daunting stretch of his broad back.

Nervously she put down the hairbrush, turned out the side-lamp and slid into the cold sheets, fully expecting to sleep immediately. But she couldn't forget the unnerving memory of Lucenzo's powerful body. She lay in an agony of suspense, wondering if he'd creep out of bed in the dark and. . . Her skin tingled and she knew that she was taut with expectation.

'Relax,' he murmured. 'Your virtue is safe.'

'I am relaxed,' she said huskily, furious that she'd sounded anything but.

To take her mind off Lucenzo, she tried to make sense of what she knew about the blackmail. Her hand strayed to the key that hung around her neck. It could be the key that Corosini had demanded in his letter. Her solicitor had said it might fit a safety-deposit box at the Venetian bank. If so, there could be some truth in Corosini's accusation.

Her body chilled at the thought. It meant she'd have to apologise to Lucenzo, to go crawling to him. Gradually her eyes drooped, her last conscious thought being of herself at Lucenzo's feet, begging for his mercy while his triumphant face came closer and closer. . .

The night seemed filled with erotic dreams. Lucenzo, herself, endless passion. She woke in the half-gloom of early morning to find her body slicked with sweat and all the bedclothes flung off, her nightdress in such a tangle that the soft creamy skin of her thighs was exposed to anyone who cared to look.

'Oh, no!' she breathed in horror.

Her head jerked around. The bed beside her was empty. She rearranged the bedclothes and tried to calm down. He probably hadn't bothered to glance at her. She bit her lip. Who was she kidding?

There was the sound of clapping and, startled, she looked up, her hair spreading like a flame on the white pillow.

'Nicely aranged. Lovely timing again, darling,' Lucenzo drawled, mimicking a stagy effusiveness. His face hardened. 'You can use the bathroom now,' he said in his normal tone.

'Thank you.' She waited for him to turn away discreetly, but realised to her concern that discretion wasn't in his nature.

Lucenzo stood towelling his blond hair, his face smooth-shaven. He looked very fresh and smart in a crisp white shirt open at the throat and charcoal-grey trousers, exquisitely cut. 'Get dressed and we'll go out.' He gave her a thoughtful look, his eyes lingering on her sleepy mouth.

'It's not seven o'clock yet!' she protested, still feeling drowsy. 'I've only been asleep a few hours.'

'I go to work early,' he replied, getting irritated as

he tried to figure out how to switch on a standard lamp. 'Get up. Or I'll get ideas again.' The light flicked on.

Her throat went dry. 'Again?' she croaked.

He threw down the towel, damp locks of hair still slicked on his forehead. 'You had one hell of a restless night,' he observed quietly.

She flushed, almost as if he could have known the part he'd played in her extraordinarily sensual dreams. 'I was hot,' she mumbled.

Lucenzo's mouth twitched. 'So I heard, so I saw.'

'Heard?' She quavered, wondering what she'd said.

'I wish my dreams gave me as much pleasure.' His voice throbbed deeply into Meredith's subconscious mind, and she felt her body leap into life. Lucenzo frowned, as if instantly aware of this, and his extraordinary knowledge of her body's behaviour was totally disconcerting, as though he owned part of it already. 'Either get up, or invite me in there with you.'

Her eyes rounded and she hugged every scrap of blanket she could around her body, making a barrier to his hot eyes. 'I told you, I'm——'

'Yes, yes,' he said impatiently. 'But for a virgin you have a highly expressive body. It knows about arousal——'

'You're making that up!' she cried defensively.

'Get up,' he growled. 'I want to satisfy one appetite at least. We'll go for breakfast when you're ready. There's a bar near by.'

'A bar?' She sat bolt upright, still clutching the blanket protectively, her face disapproving. 'At this time of day? What are you, an alcoholic? I'd rather have breakfast here. I'll even cook it. It'll save you money,' she offered generously.

'How thoughtful. But everyone has breakfast in bars. It's the custom. And in Italy we're civilised enough to serve coffee and croissants in our bars,' he said in mild reproof. 'Besides, there's no food here. I never eat in this room.'

Her gaze swept the room and she frowned. How odd. It certainly looked unlived-in. There were no personal objects around, only scattered clothes, a holdall and a sheaf of papers. Lucenzo could almost have walked in yesterday. There weren't even any photographs of his family—and in the bathroom, she remembered, there had been the minimum of male paraphernalia.

'You don't spend much time here either,' she commented.

'I move around a lot.'

He kept his eyes on her and reached for his tie. In the middle of working out whether he meant 'moving around' as in girlfriends, or 'moving around' as in innocent flat-changing, Meredith found herself quite helplessly watching every slow, calculating movement as he tied the bright madder silk around his neck.

When he'd finished, he pushed his hands into his pockets and she suddenly flushed guiltily, realising he was amused by her fascination. Her gaze shot upwards, past his curving, almost carnal mouth to lock with his glittering eyes. A small pulse began to throb erratically in the hollow of her throat and she ruefully decided that she just wasn't used to waking up and being confronted with a virile man in the process of getting dressed.

She lowered her gaze hastily and found her irrepressible sense of humour surfacing. Her lips curved into a grin. If the girls in the village ever knew she'd spent the night with an Adonis, they'd tease her unmercifully!

'How composed you are,' he drawled. 'Surely far too composed to be as innocent as you claim? Shall I find out?'

He reached forwards, bending over the bed, and drew an insolent forefinger down her cheek. Meredith meant to protest, but she was robbed of breath by the extraordinary collapse of her lungs. Odd sensations chased through her body and she found herself gasping for air. His finger paused, then touched her soft parted mouth. She began to tremble from the sheer sexual magnetism emanating from him. In an effort to escape, she pressed herself back, looking up at him in bewilderment with unblinking, deep blue eyes.

'Oh, Lucenzo,' she croaked helplessly. 'I want——'

'I know,' he ground out savagely. Both his hands grabbed at her thick, flowing hair so that she was trapped. He leant over her menacingly, pushing her deeper into the pillows. 'But this is not your lucky day.'

'But——'

'No. You won't tempt me. You've landed yourself with a man who's been wise to women's performances since the age of fourteen. They've all been my way, Meredith—tall, short, slender, curvy, and every one of them with one big fat sin motivating their pretty heads and bodies. Know what that is?'

'Sex?' she whispered.

'That at least would be human,' he growled. 'And your suggestion tells me what's on your mind at the moment.' He gave a cynical laugh at the blush which deepened the colour in her cheeks. 'It's on mine, too,' he said huskily. 'But I can control my needs because I remember what all those women wanted. Money. You'd better know now that I've always avoided every snare set out for me, even those hidden in lush undergrowth. . .' he caressed her hair lightly, his eyes sultry, and then looked down towards the swell of her breasts '. . .and innocent-looking hills and valleys.'

She quivered at the slide of his hand around the sensitive skin behind her ears, and tried to shake his hands off her hair without success. 'You're paranoid and arrogant, imagining motives that aren't there,' she said angrily, resenting the slur on her sex.

'Then perhaps I attract the wrong sort,' he hissed. 'Because that's the impression I've always been left with. Now take this as a warning. Play straight with me or I'll destroy you. Understand?' He tightened his grip on her hair. She nodded, terrified of his unexpected, violent streak. 'OK. Get up before I drag you out.'

Sullenly she massaged her scalp, giving him her coldest stare. 'That won't be necessary,' she said tightly. She slid out of bed and slipped her arms into her dressing gown, aware that his eyes were mocking her primness.

'Soft, fresh, virginal,' he murmured.

She drew the cord around her waist angrily. 'Close,' she said haughtily, tipping back her head in defiance. Her hair streamed down her back in a fury of red waves, claiming his avid eyes.

'Forget the virginal?' he suggested cynically.

'Forget the soft.'

Lucenzo's jaw set and his expression became glacial. 'We'll see,' he growled. 'I hope for your sake you're playing it straight. Or I'll show you what I do with women who try to make a fool out of me.'

'At the moment, you're doing that quite well all on your own, without my help,' she said waspishly. 'Oh, heavens! This room needs a change of air,' she muttered, ashamed that he'd goaded her into being catty.

She fiddled with the catches on the shutters and folded them back, her anger cooling at the haunting, distant sound of a boatman singing. The window was directly above a canal, and she opened the casements wider so that she could hear better. The boatman appeared through the morning gloom, poling a small gondola filled with fresh vegetables.

'*Bella, bella*!' he called to her, when he saw her leaning precariously out, her hair flowing like a red waterfall over her shoulders. After Lucenzo's harsh treatment of her, it was wonderful to be appreciated.

'Thank you!' she smiled happily. '*Grazie!*'

'Careful!' Lucenzo's hands gripped her waist.

She remained very still, marvelling secretly at the strength of his restraining hands. It occurred to her that he could tip her out of the wndow without any effort at all, and she shrank back. But that brought her into contact with his hot, hard body, and she strained away again, aware of his sharp intake of breath at her quivering shudder. The gondolier sang a few liquid golden bars of a love song while she listened in rapture.

'You can let me go,' she said stiffly, turning her head slightly, when the sound of the song had become only an echo.

'I could.'

He spun her roughly around. In consternation, she tried to make out why the hard, grim mouth had become so appealing. The little curl at each corner, the extravagant sweep up to the two high peaks and the dent above. . . She blinked. He'd taken her hand and his mouth was brushing her fingers, and for a crazy moment she actually wished that those warm, soft lips were on hers instead.

'Lucenzo,' she whispered apprehensively.

He touched the bright, brash scarlet of her hair. His gaze lifted to where her breasts were swelling beneath the soft material of her gown. Meredith trembled, overwhelmed by the sheer proximity of him, the heat and vitality of his body filling her with an unholy excitement. She gulped, looking down, and her lips parted as she tried to speak.

'What big blue eyes you have,' husked Lucenzo. 'And what soft, kissable lips.' His eyes suddenly narrowed. 'All the better to catch me with?' he muttered.

She gasped indignantly. 'Yes! I had them specially done!'

He grinned and brushed her hair back with fingers which lingered on her brow. And somehow Meredith knew that he wouldn't be as easy to brush off, or to coax, or to divert with jokes as the other young men she'd fended off.

Lucenzo had a ruthless streak that was absent in her country boyfriends. He'd take whatever he wanted because he was a man, and in this country men thought they ruled supreme. He deliberately shifted forwards so that their bodies were lined up intimately, her soft breasts rising and falling against his firm, masculine chest.

'I find you very exciting,' he said huskily. 'I thought I'd let you know.' And then he let her go.

Ablaze with fiery emotions, Meredith walked self-consciously to the bathroom under Lucenzo's critical eyes. She'd always prided herself on her inner strength. It looked as if she'd need every ounce.

Once on the streets, Lucenzo raised the collar of his heavy black coat, huddling into it. Like a spy in a B movie, Meredith thought in amazement. It was almost as if he was trying to hide. Perhaps he was ashamed of striding the dark wintry streets with a woman in a tea-cosy. A small giggle slipped from her lips. His golden head whipped around and she was blasted by a pair of fierce eyes above the concealing collar.

'You have the oddest sense of humour,' he frowned.

'At least I have one. Is everything in Venice frozen except for the canals?' she asked wickedly.

'Solid,' he answered, his voice muffled.

She sighed. There was no easing this intractable man. 'No signs of any future thaw?' she enquired with a forced brightness.

He gave her a sour look. 'Things will improve in a few days. You'll be gone by then,' he said pointedly.

'If I haven't died of hunger first,' she said with asperity. 'We've passed five places selling coffee and pastries already, including the one just around the corner from your flat.'

'Maybe they're too expensive,' he said sardonically.

'Or maybe you don't want to be seen with me. . .' Meredith glared. He'd begun to scowl before she had even finished her sentence. 'What a snob you are,' she accused. 'Seduction's OK, walking down the street isn't! Or are you sulking because I rejected you?'

'Don't make me angry,' he warned in a low tone. 'Don't taunt me. I'm not in the mood.'

Meredith recognised the bottom line and she said no more. Lucenzo strode relentlessly on. They came to a large square, dazzling white from swirling snow-drifts. Someone had laid out knee-high duckboards to cross the snow, and Lucenzo shot out an imperious hand to help her on to the low platform.

She chose to accept his good manners at face value. 'Thank you.' She smiled pleasantly. Her small hand grasped his, and he drew her up on to the low walkway.

'You go on, I'll catch up,' he said, his voice stifled by the thick wool collar, blown by the wind across his mouth. 'That's the bar over there.'

A biting wind had blown up and ruffled his fair hair as he nodded towards the brightly lit bar on the other side of the square. Then his cold hand released hers. Left to fend for herself, Meredith slowly crossed the square and then turned.

He was gently coaxing an old lady on to the duck-boards, and his elaborate care and concern made Meredith think better of him. He couldn't be all that ruthless and cold-hearted if he respected his elders, she mused, her spirits lifting.

Thoughtfully she watched his elegant figure in the well-cut black coat, his hair streaming in the wind and shining like molten gold in the morning light. Slowly, as if driven, and knowing full well what she was doing, Meredith pulled off her hat and released her own hair again as he neared the end of the duckboards, still gently guiding the old lady and chatting to her courteously.

'*Tante grazie*,' said the woman to Lucenzo. She held out her hand regally, her strong-boned features proud and confident.

'*Prego*, *signora*,' he answered with a warm smile.

Then his face chilled down. His eyes were on Meredith, who was framed against the peeling ochre

wall, her flame-burst of hair a startling contrast to her
pale cream skin and the delicate snowflakes which lay
scattered on her head like confetti. And she was
smiling warmly too, her whole face sweet and happy,
because it had been a charming sight—Lucenzo
bowing with old-world charm over the old lady's hand,
and the softened chocolate of his eyes, which iced up
immediately they met Meredith's, and the gentleness
of her expression turned to bewilderment.

It seemed odd that he loathed her with such intensity
and yet had made a pass at her. Meredith's brain
ticked over rapidly and she came to one undeniable
conclusion. His natural, male hunger had driven him
to reach out for her. She'd been there at the time he'd
wanted a woman. But he hated himself for being
drawn to her, however briefly, because he was person-
ally involved. . .

'This Corosini,' she blurted out, as it all became
crystal-clear. Lucenzo claimed he would defend his
family to the end. Therefore. . .'You're related to
him, aren't you?'

Lucenzo's brows flew up. 'What an extraordinary
deduction!' he snapped scathingly.

'I don't see why. It would make sense,' she argued.
'You said you were devoted to your family. I could
understand your animosity towards me if you were a
cousin or something.'

He stiffened. 'A. . .cousin?'

'Corosini's cousin,' she explained patiently. 'He'd
be more likely to confide in you then, if you were
more than just his banker. And apart from moments
when you wanted. . .when. . .' she shot her chin up
aggressively at his amused look '. . .when you were
after sex,' she said, driven to boldness by his taunting
mockery, 'you've been hostile and unwelcoming to
me.'

Meredith met Lucenzo's hard, stony eyes, and shivered as a strong gust of icy wind sent her hair in all
directions.

'What an extraordinary imagination you have,' he muttered. 'And you've made yourself cold. You should have gone in and not waited for me.' He pushed open the door to the bar. 'Hurry up. There's no point in the people inside getting frozen as well.' He gave her a push.

Meredith staggered a little and he grabbed her. She felt the steel strength of his arms around her and her skin quivered from the warmth of his breath on her cheek before he released her as if she might contaminate him.

His extreme distaste at being seen to touch her in public was utterly humiliating. Miserably she handed him her coat at his frosty request, her chastened eyes seeing the annoyed glares from those nearest the door.

'I'm sorry, it's terribly cold, isn't it? Please forgive me,' she begged everyone contritely.

This time, her directness must have been disarming, because there was an answering murmur as if the people in the bar knew what she'd said. Her anxious figure was bathed in the warmth of smiles and dark, twinkling glances.

Instantly happier, she stood beside Lucenzo at the counter, absorbing the atmosphere. It was everything she loved—loads of friendly people, talking at the tops of their voices like a big family party. Most were men, drinking coffees and brandies. Great plates of sticky, sweet cakes and pastries were being consumed with tremendous gusto, and one man appeared to be eating a huge slab of pizza.

'Alcohol for breakfast! And seafood pizza! What a way to start the day!' she marvelled, while Lucenzo cautiously returned several deferential nods with an inclination of his fair head. 'I admire their digestions. Are these people customers of your bank?' she asked curiously.

'No. They're mostly boatmen.'

'I expect they need something warm inside them, with this weather,' she said sympathetically.

'Yes. It's darn cold, taking a scow up the canal. Coffee?' Lucenzo asked grudgingly.

Her mouth drooped at the corners. She'd been all set to enjoy being here, and had momentarily forgotten how taciturn her minder could be. 'I'd rather have tea, please,' she said politely.

'My God!' muttered Lucenzo, looking heavenwards. 'Tea! Be it on your own head.'

'I'd prefer it in the cup,' she retorted drily, and was rewarded with the faintest tremor of Lucenzo's mobile mouth. Promising. She'd get him to smile if it was the last thing she did! 'I have a terrible sweet tooth. How much are those doughnut things?' she asked him more cheerfully.

'*Fritole*?' He followed her hungry gaze to the pyramid of tiny doughnuts, piled up in an embossed brass dish. 'Order what you like. Have a brandy. Spend as much as you want—the bank's paying. Ham, pizza, pastries, wine. . .' He spoke rapidly to the barman in beautiful, lilting Italian and leaned against the counter, his remote eyes fixed on the man deftly operating the espresso machine.

'No thanks. I'm not running up a large bill unnecessarily. You can rook your employers for as much as you want if you must, but I pay my own way,' she said firmly.

'Clever Miss Prim,' he murmured, swivelling his enigmatic gaze in her direction.

She intentionally misinterpreted his scathing remark. 'Aren't I,' she agreed blithely. 'My parents might have spent every penny they earned on helping their out-of-work friends, but Gran brought me up to be thrifty and never to get into debt.' She inhaled the aroma of his thick black coffee and looked with some doubt at her murky cup of tea.

'Admirable,' Lucenzo said, his mouth mocking. 'I think I've got the message. You're incorruptible. But the bank won't crash merely because I've bought you a cup of tea and a few Carnival cakes.'

He sipped his coffee and then poured water from a
carafe into a glass. Meredith tried her tea and wrinkled
her nose up in distaste. Without a word, Lucenzo
offered her a jug of coffee and flicked a quick finger at
the alert barman, who provided her with a fresh cup.
The coffee smelt and tasted rich, quite unlike the
freeze-dried brand she used at home. Copying
Lucenzo, she sipped the coffee and then the water,
discovering the pleasure of the contrasting tastes.

'This is wonderful,' she said appreciatively.

'Of course. Venetian water is the best in the world,'
Lucenzo claimed expansively. 'And so is the coffee.
We've been importing it for centuries. It's far superior
to anywhere else.'

Meredith smiled at his pride. She sensed a similar,
blissful confidence about everyone around her: the
barman, cheerfully serving his customers with a lightning speed, the boatmen and labourers, and the shop
girls, who seemed completely sure of themselves and
unashamedly exuberant.

She caught the barman's eye and beamed contentedly at his hot red face as he sipped iced water, taking
a brief rest. 'Do you speak English?' she asked eagerly.
He nodded. 'I bet you've done a day's work already.
You must get up very early.' She smiled warmly.

'*Si*. And my wife. She make the food. Now she do
the *pasta e fagioli*,' he said, the words tripping lyrically
off his tongue. 'Pasta and bean soup. You like?'

'Sounds wonderful,' she said solemnly, her face
gentle and friendly.

'Eh, you try,' he coaxed. 'Is ready. *Allora*, with a
leetle Campari——'

'Oh, no! I couldn't! Not at this time——'

'*Signorina*, with this cold day, you like to be warm
in here.' He slammed a huge fist into his large stomach
and she laughed merrily, obediently accepting his
ceremonial presentation of the soup, and watching
wide-eyed while he poured a generous measure of
Campari into it.

'I'll fall off the stool!' she protested.

'So, enjoy. We catch.'

Half the bar seemed to be indulgently waiting for her opinion. She sipped, blinked, and grinned, then spooned up every bit, wiping the bowl clean with some freshly baked bread that the barman handed her.

'Fantastic!' she proclaimed, her face bright pink.

Applause rang out, and she twirled around to acknowledge it in demure delight, clapping the barman—and then being crushed against the ample bosom of the barman's wife.

'*Bella*, *bellissima*!' cried the woman, freeing the laughing Meredith.

'She says you are beautiful,' murmured Lucenzo, and Meredith's cheeks pinkened at his slow gaze.

'*Mi piacciono questi capelli*,' cried the woman, unabashed at openly admiring the red and gold strands of Meredith's hair.

'Your hair gives her pleasure.'

Quivers of movement, like trickles of electricity, danced over Meredith's skin at the sound of his velvety voice. The woman inclined her head politely to Lucenzo, who was quietly watching Meredith's reactions, and disappeared back into the kitchen. Lucenzo turned away, and the tension miraculously left, though the warmth stayed in her body to remind her.

She settled once more to enjoying the atmosphere, feeling rather hyped up. 'I *love* it here,' she said enthusiastically, seeing that Lucenzo had relaxed to some extent and was actually exchanging a few pleasantries with one or two people. 'It's noisy and carefree,' she mused. 'People are affectionate. It's like my childhood years.'

'Lucky you,' he said sourly.

A veil came over her eyes. 'I miss Mum and Dad so much,' she mumbled, a catch in her voice. No one had hugged her as the woman had, for years. Compared with her exuberant father and her uninhibited mother,

Gran had been a little restrained. Her hand touched her breast to stem the physical pain there.

Lines of strain appeared around Lucenzo's mouth. Its high peaks flattened and the sensual curves ironed out in grim response to her confidence. 'Cut out the sentimental references. I'm not interested,' he growled.

Meredith abruptly stopped confiding her emotions to him and nibbled the doughnut forlornly. It tasted of candied peel and nuts, and she was reaching for another one when she saw that Lucenzo's head had lifted at the sound of a child's piping tones. Intrigued, she followed his gaze. His dark, infinitely unreadable eyes were glued to a man solemnly adjusting the ruff of a child in a clown's costume.

She held her breath at the look of tenderness spreading slowly over Lucenzo's face. Enchanted, she too watched the sweet-faced boy who was chattering excitedly while his fond father plied him with Carnival cakes.

She had needed an ice-breaker. Perhaps this was it. 'A father's love is very special,' she began softly.

Lucenzo flinched. 'Is it?' he said abruptly. 'I never knew mine.'

'Oh!' she cried, with a rush of genuine, deep-felt sympathy. She touched his arm gently and met his puzzled eyes. 'I'm sorry. How awful. And I thought I was unlucky,' she said huskily. 'My parents died when I was a teenager, you see. But they loved me so passionately that I had a secure base to my life.'

'Didn't your mother resent your arrival on the scene? A baby must have brought a grinding halt to her career?' he enquired slowly.

'Not for long!' grinned Meredith. 'I went where she went. She bounced back with renewed vigour.'

'That figures. You're like her, are you?'

'I do bounce,' she admitted, her expression far-away. 'My arrival thrilled Mother. She'd given up all hope of having children, you see. They were getting on a bit when I was born.' Lucenzo's eyes had strayed to the child, who was contentedly wrapped in his father's embrace. 'I love children,' she said softly, seeing that Lucenzo did too. 'I worked in a crèche before I had to give that up to look after Gran. It was a heavenly job, working with children. I understood how Mother felt when she knew she was pregnant at long last. Imagine how sad it must be, if you want babies and can't have them.'

Lucenzo swirled the water in his glass, his eyes hooded. Meredith watched the long, well-manicured fingers gripping the glass until his joints showed white and she thought for one crazy moment that it was going to break into shards. She wondered what hidden secrets were stored away in that private, well-guarded brain of his. Something disturbed him; something to do with children—and she was bursting to know what that was.

'Childless couples can adopt,' he said flatly.

'Oh, I know,' she agreed, speaking softly. 'And I'd adopt, rather than not have a family at all. But it's not *quite* the same as your very own flesh and blood, is it?' Staring into the distance and thus blissfully unaware that his jaw had clenched ominously, she plunged on. 'Mother was ecstatic to be pregnant.' She smiled absently. 'So much so that she told the entire matinée audience of a Noel Coward play! But she'd forgotten to tell Father first—he was her manager, you know.'

'Why should I know?' he muttered

'Well,' she continued, engrossed in her story, 'he brought the house down by flying on to the stage like a whirlwind and sweeping Mother off her feet!' She chuckled. 'Everyone cried buckets.'

It was a tale her mother had told fondly, over and over again, and every time her lovely face had been suffused with remembered joy. That joy was reflected in Meredith's face now.

Lucenzo ground his teeth. 'I have no wish to be

regaled with reminiscences about your childhood,' he said scathingly.

'I'm sorry,' she apologised, recognising the pain behind his irritation. Her stories hurt because he'd experienced nothing like her happiness. She hesitated, and then decided to confide in him. 'I understand your feelings.'

'I doubt it.'

'I do. You see, now Gran has gone I have no one. And I feel so empty, so alone. I wish. . . Do you know, I long for a family more than anything in the world?' she blurted out with an intense yearning.

Lucenzo scowled heavily. 'Get married.'

'No, it's not that. . . I mean aunts and uncles, cousins, a gang of nephews and nieces——'

'We're leaving,' he said abruptly, not touched by her wistful dreams in the slightest. 'I've given you breakfast. You'll get nothing more from me. So you might as well go to the information office in San Marco and book yourself on the next flight out of here. You'll never find Corosini on your own.'

Something made her bite her tongue. She'd intended to tell him she wanted to open the safety-deposit box, but it occurred to her that he might put obstacles in her way. 'It would be almost impossible,' she agreed quietly. 'You think I should go home?' She flicked back a hank of heavy hair.

'I think that you and Corosini would be better off if you forgot each other's existence,' muttered Lucenzo.

'I see. . .' Meredith knew she shouldn't sound too keen to fall in with his plans. 'I could have a bit of a wander round before I go,' she suggested. For the first time in her life, she had avoided the straight truth, and her words sat uncomfortably on her conscience. But this was important. 'Where is your bank? Could I walk with you and then find my own way back to San Marco?'

'If you must,' he said grudgingly. Yet Meredith detected a faint smile of triumph on his face. 'Pay the man at the till, would you?' he said, counting out some notes. 'This is the right money. Here's the bill. I just want to have a word with someone.'

He moved over to a group of boatmen sitting beneath a large gilt mirror. Meredith queued up at the till, studying the amount on the bill, and automatically checked what he'd given her while she was waiting. She frowned, and checked again, her eyes widening in amazement. There was about five hundred pounds too much. For a banker he was pretty careless with money! Glancing over, she saw he was deep in conversation, so she found the right amount and paid. He collected his coat and draped it over one shoulder.

'Lucenzo,' she chided, 'you gave me *far* too much! Look!'

He seemed almost disappointed to be handed back the wad of notes. 'This is mine? I'm amazed at your honesty. You could have pocketed that quite easily.'

She looked puzzled. 'But it's yours!'

He studied her for several seconds, as if baffled. She lifted an enquiring eyebrow, wondering if it would have suited his purposes if she'd said nothing, because he could then have accused her of theft. Her mouth thinned and she hardened her heart to him.

'Come with me,' he said, without expression on his face, his voice or his body to tell her what he was thinking. 'I'm going in the direction of the Rialto Bridge. You can take the *Accelerato* back. That's the slow boat, down the Grand Canal,' he explained. 'It goes from side to side, stopping at every landing point so you'll have a good—and cheap—view of all the buildings along the canal.'

'Lovely,' she said solemnly. 'I look forward to that.' And when they reached his bank, she thought, she'd broach the subject of the safety-deposit box. Her stomach flipped with nerves. She'd come all this way to find out the truth about her family, and now she was close to the answer and she wasn't sure she really wanted to know.

CHAPTER FOUR

THE Grand Canal was packed with craft of all kinds: little passenger ferries groaning with commuters, barges loaded with crates of fresh vegetables, floating cranes, skiffs, garbage boats. . . Meredith soon forgot everything but the endlessly fascinating unfolding scene.

'All this hustle and bustle makes me feel exhilarated!' She smiled, excitement bubbling inside her as she perched precariously on the edge of a jetty. It was bobbing up and down from the wash of a smart motorboat which had swept by, filled with haughty-looking Venetians with faces so medieval that they could have stepped straight from the history books.

'It's the rush-hour,' Lucenzo said languidly, watching her with something resembling vague indulgence.

Meredith flung him an eager glance, enthralled by the noise, the snow, the funereal gondolas bobbing in the water. 'Aren't you dazzled by it every day of your life?' she said enthusiastically.

'Thrilled.'

She ignored his assumed air of uninterest. She knew perfectly well he'd been trying to hide the fact that he'd come alive as the streets had filled with people. He was as energised by it all as she was.

'I don't know how those people can read newspapers when they're chugging past scenery like this!' She waved an expansive arm at the commuters on a passing ferry.

'Beauty palls after a while—unless, of course, there's something deeper beneath the surface to hold the interest,' observed Lucenzo laconically.

'It certainly does,' she agreed, wondering how many beauties had disappointed him. 'But there's much more to Venice than meets the eye, isn't there? It's more than just beautiful wrapping, more than lovely façades.'

'Perceptive of you,' he commented, with a faint tinge of interest in his dark eyes. 'What do you see beyond the mask it presents to visitors?'

'Mysteries,' she said softly, scanning the tall windows and the shutters that kept the world out and passions securely locked in. 'All this show and pageantry. . .it's a front, for the real emotions and dramas of the ordinary people inside. It holds the answer to my secret somewhere. There must be other secrets, and it would be fascinating discovering them——'

'What do you mean, "other secrets"?' he asked, closing in on her shoulder.

'I don't know!' she grinned, absorbed in watching a group of beautifully dressed Venetians stepping into a gondola. It seemed to be some kind of ferry, because they were being poled across from one side of the canal to the other—while they remained standing, like people on a packed London bus. Her eyes twinkled with the fun of it all. 'Venice is old enough to have thousands of secrets: vendettas, love-children, frauds—especially if it was the banking capital of the world for hundreds of years.' She glanced at him saucily. 'You bankers are full of intrigue and schemes—Lucenzo!' she warned huskily, as his arms came around her. 'What are you doing?'

'Responding,' he answered, with a heart-stopping smile. It was also highly predatory.

Her eyes widened. 'To what?'

'You, of course. You're going to leave me soon, and I'll regret it forever more if I never kiss you properly. You're very beautiful, very provocative, when you look at me with those flirting eyes.' His arms tightened imperceptibly, effectively trapping her.

'I wasn't flirting,' she said quickly, fighting to keep a decent space between their bodies. 'I was talking. . .' His head angled and Meredith's battle began against

the jolt of desire that the simple action had created.
'About. . .' His lips parted. She clenched her jaw to
kill the sultry languor that was stealing over her at the
sight of his thick lashes lying in two black arcs on his
gilded cheekbones. 'Secrets!' she cried, triumphantly
grasping the word.

'Meredith,' he whispered longingly.

'What——?' She gulped, barely capable of denying
herself the inevitable. 'I want to talk to you——'

'Waste of time.' His voice rasped each word on to
her pouting mouth, caressing it with sweet warmth.
'We don't have long if you're going.'

A small frown drew her brows together and she
arched back to look at him with as much objectivity as
she could summon up. He seemed determined to
emphasise the fact that she was leaving. 'What are you
up to?' she asked hoarsely.

'No good,' he said cynically. His hands found places
on her spine which seemed to hunger for his expert
touch. She drew her head back further. 'Say goodbye
to me Italian style,' he coaxed huskily. 'A lingering,
never-forgotten farewell.'

Another time, another place, she thought, and she
might have done. But, suspicious of his motives, she
tested his sincerity. 'I might not go just yet. . .' For a
split second he was unable to hide his anger, and she
felt disappointed that he was only manipulating her.

'You're staying?' His eyes gleamed.

He slid his hand to her hip, where it gently rotated
in a maddeningly sensual rhythm. He bent her supple
body back; she took one look over her shoulder and
saw nothing but fast-flowing black water.

'Don't!' she wailed. 'You'll push me in the canal!'
She twisted her head from one side to the other, trying
to avoid the determined approach of his sensual
mouth, aware that she was in no position to move an
inch. 'You brute!' she whispered, her lips unbearably
close to his. 'If I try to escape, I'm in danger of falling
in.'

His eyebrow quivered, registering admiration. 'So you will,' he growled. 'You'd better co-operate, hadn't you?' he added, with a sinister undertone in his voice.

'I'll scream!' she mumbled, straining back so hard that her neck ached.

'You'd be in the canal by then.'

'Oh, you wouldn't dare!' she gasped.

'Try me.'

He played with her, letting his grasp slip so that she almost toppled backwards, then saving her by pulling her roughly back into his body. She clung to him, terrified—furious because he was showing her that he was in total command of the situation. And she was only just gathering breath to protest when his lips eventually captured hers, their sweetness instantly filling her with a warm, deep pleasure. She gave a little moan of private enjoyment and reluctantly slid her hands up to his face. She put her palms against his cheeks, forcing his head back, her unhappy eyes pleading with him.

'No, Lucenzo!' she scolded huskily.

'I've got you,' he murmured silkily, his mouth exploring hers with a thoroughness that made her head spin. 'You won't fall.' He gave a private smile. 'Not till tonight, that is.'

'Ohh!' she gasped, shocked by the implications of what he'd said. 'No! I won't be staying in your flat. Not now—I couldn't!'

'Oh, dear. This *is* goodbye, then. You're definitely going home,' he sighed with a show of sorrow, easing back a fraction, his dark eyes liquid and watchful.

How could she lie to him? If he weren't so close, she'd be able to think of avoiding action, but. . .

'N-no, not exactly——'

Her tremulous voice was stopped by his mouth closing on hers in a deep, sensual kiss which rocked her off her feet until she felt there were no bones in her body at all. Her moans were ignored. Lucenzo's hands roamed tantalisingly, smoothing over the curves of her arching spine and taking pleasure in the deep indent of her waist. It was wonderful. She loved it.

She mumbled beneath his mouth when his fingers pressed hard into her firm buttocks, and she felt a hot flame burn where his hand had rested, her mouth, her body, her mind all whirling with the incredible sensation that his unprovoked assault was arousing.

'If you stay, Meredith, if you go anywhere in Venice, I'll find you and lay siege to you.'

His eyes seared hers with a glowing intensity that excited her. She'd long dreamed of being desired by a man whose need was so overwhelming that he would do anything to be with her. But Lucenzo was a charlatan, she reminded herself. Behind that passionate face lay indifference.

'You can't mean that,' she whispered.

'No?' He smiled menacingly. His head closed in, filling her vision, his tongue lightly tracing the meeting of her lips. She gasped from a sudden tearing hunger deep inside her and he smiled with his mouth but not his eyes. 'Stay or go. You want me or you don't. Decide *now*. Well?'

'I—I——' She gulped and grabbed the intrusive fingers which had begun to slide to her breast. 'You're behaving outrageously! Don't!' she said faintly.

Dimly she heard the pounding of her own pulses in her ears. She couldn't believe this was happening to her. He was treating her like a cheap pick-up. Her eyes filled with a hot prickling that he should humiliate her in public, with half of Venice floating by. And the tears were for herself too, because her treacherous, sensation-loving body had enjoyed—even wanted— his touch. She shut her eyes in shame.

'You'll go?' he asked harshly.

A sprinkling of hot tears fell on to his exploring lips. For a moment he savoured their saltiness and then he seemed to register that her body was being racked with sobs. His hands fell away and he moved back, his face totally inscrutable.

'Cenzo! *Cos'è?*' came a shocked cry.

He spun around, livid with a sudden anger, twin glinting lights of glittering black beneath his hooded lids. '*Non lo so*,' he grated, passing a distracted hand through his blond hair. '*Non lo so*,' he repeated harshly. Meredith miserably eyed the bevy of beautiful women who'd appeared, apparently friends of his, but the tears began to blind her and their faces blurred. '*Mi lasce in pace*,' he ground out.

'*A presto. Ciao*,' said a woman's voice doubtfully.

'What were you saying?' moaned Meredith.

'I told them to leave me in peace,' he said harshly.

'Leave *you* in peace?' she exclaimed. 'What about me? How could you?' she wept, shaken by a deep shame. And then she felt Lucenzo's arms around her again and she lashed out furiously, weak with distress but trying frantically to fend him off.

'*Tranquilo, tranquilo*,' he was saying impatiently.

She froze, her whole body numb. A sharp, cruel memory had slid into her mind: her father, calming her when she'd cried hysterically at the death of her new kitten. *Tranquilo*, he'd said. Be calm. She went ice-cold and her limbs felt like lead weights. Because now she knew her father had spoken in Italian.

'Oh, dear heaven!' she whispered.

Her father had used the word instinctively. He'd been upset. But that word had come naturally to him. Meredith lifted her tear-stained face. Her father had had a link with Italy. The thought drummed into her relentlessly, rooting her to the spot.

'Meredith! Meredith!' said Lucenzo fiercely, shaking her.

Slowly she focused on him. 'Oh, Lucenzo!' she said brokenly.

She found herself unable to speak with the fear that clutched at her, the worrying possibility that her whole life had been built on a lie. Her mind sifted the evidence. Father had always dressed beautifully. He had adored good food, good wine, music, beautiful things. . . The doubts were beginning to mount up alarmingly. Maybe Lucenzo had good reason to treat her with contempt. Maybe her family had extorted money. . . Her legs gave way suddenly, and Lucenzo's arms came up to hold her limp body.

'Can you be for real?' he muttered.

'Please, I can't——' She sought refuge in his comforting chest, too numb to explain.

There was some shuffling and the sound of people speaking, as if a small crowd was gathering, but all she could do was place her head against his shirt front and sob.

'It wasn't that embarrassing,' he rumbled. His chest expanded with irritation. 'OK. If you're determined to cry, you're doing it in private. I'm taking you to the bank,' he muttered in her ear, his voice reverberating through her body. 'It's in the Street of the Goldsmiths near by. It's a while till we open for trading, so you can have a good howl if you want.' Meredith thought she detected a gentler tone creeping into his words, and felt comforted, but then he spoilt it all. 'Till then, do me a favour and stem the flow,' he snapped.

Pride, not obedience, made her do what he requested, and she was glad of his support. It was ironic, especially as it was he who was causing her world to come crashing about her head.

He protected her like a lover, shielding her from curious eyes as they climbed the steep steps of the Rialto bridge with its shops on either side. An increase in the noise level and glimpses of exotic vegetables told her that they were in a market street, and it seemed to the over-sensitive Meredith that Lucenzo was almost continually returning greetings and brushing off sympathetic offers of help.

At last he unlocked a heavily carved door, and after a moment Meredith saw that he'd led her into a large office with plaster frescos and a glorious ceiling of painted angels hung with gilded chandeliers.

Stony-faced Lucenzo seated her in an opulently

covered settle and knelt down in front of her, holding her hands and looking thunderous. 'I thought it could be turned off, like a tap,' he said sardonically. Meredith winced. 'You're good enough an actress to be invited to our *Fenice* theatre.'

'I don't like your methods,' she said resentfully.

His eyes glimmered. 'I use any method to get what I want, when I want it.'

'Does that apply across the board?' she asked tremulously. 'In business and with women?'

A small smile played around his mouth, and Meredith felt the increasingly familiar swoop of her stomach. 'I never fail to get what I want,' he said with unnervingly quiet confidence. 'Either in business or in love.'

'Then get ready for a shock,' she snapped.

Lucenzo looked at her steadily. 'I haven't stopped trying yet.'

Meredith slicked her tongue over her lips and her body jerked at the hunger in Lucenzo's eyes. He put his hand on her knee. 'Would you get me some water, please?' she asked, managing to disguise her nerves.

His smile was mocking. '*Certo.*'

She watched his tall figure stride over the marble floor. When he'd gone, she leaned back and tried to calm herself down. She had too much to think about, too many problems. *Tranquilo*, she thought, and her face tightened with agitation. *Tranquilo*. She gave an inner groan of despair. She wanted a link between her father and Venice like she wanted a hole in the head. The implications were too awful to contemplate. She groaned aloud.

'Drink this,' came Lucenzo's stern voice. He handed her the glass of iced water and began to pace up and down restlessly.

She sipped the drink and watched him from under her lashes. In this magnificent room, he looked as if he belonged, his face and bearing as noble as any aristocrat's. Apprehensively, she worried that she might have taken on more than she could cope with. How could she expect to take on the powerful Lucenzo Salviati—a man with centuries of trickery in his blood—and come out top?

Lucenzo paused, frowned at the baroque timepiece on the desk and set the clock by his Rolex. 'This is your office, isn't it?' she asked in a small voice. 'Are you the manager here?'

He came to a halt, his profile haughty before the leaded window. The sun shone through an elaborate crest of arms in coloured glass, with the lion of Venice rampant above a flurry of plumes and a Latin motto, the glass throwing dark Harlequin patterns on to his expressionless face.

'Not the manager.' He seemed to be coming to a decision to tell her something, and she waited with her heart thudding in her chest. His eyes slanted to hers. 'I own the bank.'

Meredith was quite still, staring up at him, wondering how many other secrets lay behind that implacable façade. Her body began to tremble. If he was that important, then Corosini himself must wield even more power than Lucenzo.

'If you'd only told me——' she began.

'Does it make a difference?' he asked cynically.

'Yes.'

He lifted his head proudly, the sun turning his hair to white-gold and shadowing his face. 'I want you,' he said softly. 'If you stay, I'll have you—that's a promise. Is that what you want too? You're poor, I'm rich——'

'Are you suggesting a purchase?' she flung at him.

'A deal.'

'Dear heaven! You're pushing me to the limit,' she whispered, cringing into the brocade settle and holding her drink in front of her defensively.

'Yes,' he replied softly. 'It's my way.'

'It's disgusting!' she cried. 'It makes no difference

who or what you are. If you're not the man I love and
if you don't love me, then I am not available.'

The silence lengthened as Lucenzo surveyed her,
and she knew intuitively that he was debating whether
to pursue her or not, wondering if she was worth
teasing any longer and perhaps forming some other
devilish plan. She steeled herself. There was much to
come, she knew.

'OK.' He strode to his desk and reached for the
telephone. 'I give in. Before I regret the temporary
arrival of my better nature, you'd better let me make
a few calls and see what I can do to get you home
today.'

Meredith thought quickly. Lucenzo didn't have a
better nature. He seemed unusually anxious to get rid
of her, and that wasn't due to his embarrassment at
being rejected and shown up in front of his friends as
a bully. It certainly wasn't because he was trying to
save her from a Fate Worse than Death. She allowed
herself a small smile. And decided to fight on despite
the problems.

'Just give me a moment,' she begged, letting him
hear the tremor in her voice. His hand wavered, and
she noticed the steel discipline which made him drop
the phone back in its cradle and wait while she sipped
the water. 'I'm still a bit shaky,' she said truthfully.
With an effort, she made herself look with interest
around his office, though it was really beautifully
furnished and her initial pretence changed to frank
admiration. 'Your bank seems to be doing well,' she
remarked.

'Terribly. You like the exotic?' He smiled absently,
stroking the carved Moor's head on a *torchère*. 'The
bank made shipments from Timbuktu in the Middle
Ages, when African gold was at its finest.'

She wanted to know more, but forced herself to
manipulate him. 'You must enjoy working in such
opulence.' His mouth twisted and he began to thumb
through the telephone directory, his patience appar-

ently wavering. 'Apart from the boring bits, like opening up, checking the vaults and so on,' she mused, holding her breath to see if he took the bait. She was learning Venetian wiliness, she thought wryly.

'I don't mind that.' He was only half listening, engrossed in tapping out the telephone number.

'Good. Since you have the keys and I'm a customer, I want to be taken to the vault, please,' she said in a loud, clear voice, her heart hammering with apprehension.

He froze. '*Customer*? The vault?' he barked. 'There's nothing down there——'

'Except the safety-deposit boxes,' she finished.

The phone slipped from Lucenzo's fingers to the highly polished desk with a clatter. He swore fluently. But when he looked up again the mask had hidden any inner reaction, and she realised how skilled he was in covering up his emotions. 'It's not a tourist sight——'

'I'm not sight-seeing,' she said firmly. 'I'm doing business.'

'What business could you possibly have in our vaults?' he asked softly.

Soft his speech might be, but Meredith felt she was being speared by the twin daggers of his eyes. Looming over his huge desk, he took on a frightening aspect. For some reason, he didn't want her to check out the vault. She had to keep her wits about her in the next few minutes.

'I have inherited the contents of a safety-deposit box. I believe it's one of yours.'

Lucenzo's composure wavered fractionally. 'Your authority?'

'Probates,' she said, producing them from her bag. 'For my parents and for my grandmother.' Meredith lifted her chin to stiffen her nerves. 'On Gran's statements was an annual debit for a safe custody charge at the Banco D'Oro. My local bank manager said that means she'd been renting a deposit box. I want to see what's inside it.'

'But you need a key to the box. And you said yourself that this Corosini business was a mistake, a computer error.' His eyes narrowed at her expression of utter confidence.

Her head tipped to one side. She licked her dry lips, afraid of what the next few minutes would reveal. 'That's true. Nevertheless, I have a key and it could open one of your boxes.'

'*Gesù*!' exclaimed Lucenzo. 'You said you had nothing that had belonged to your father!' he accused savagely.

'Father?' she queried, frowning. 'I thought the key was Gran's—it was with her things. As far as I knew, she'd either thrown away or burnt Dad's possessions——'

'She—*what*?' Lucenzo leant forward, his piercing dark gaze fixed intently on Meredith.

'She got rid of everything. Not one thing was left,' she whispered unhappily.

Lucenzo's eyes closed briefly and then snapped open again to reveal a hot, blazing fury. 'The bitch! Why, in the name of God, *why*?'

Meredith started. 'It was Father's wishes,' she frowned, baffled by his reaction. 'I saw the will. Gran destroyed everything the minute she heard Father had died.'

'Dear God!' he breathed.

Meredith's eyes filled. She bit her lip. 'I wish I had *something*!' she cried passionately. 'It's as if he's been wiped off the face of the earth!'

'Extraordinary!' muttered Lucenzo, obviously appalled. 'To have gone to such lengths to destroy——' Meredith heard his muttered expletive, but he said no more—just began to pace the room with a restless air as if he were in a prison and desperate to get out.

Meredith had stiffened. She stared at Lucenzo in consternation, sitting erect in the chair, unnerved by a terrible idea that had come into her head. 'You don't

think. . .there could have been something. . .*dark* in
his past that he was trying to hide, do you?'

He didn't answer for a moment, and it seemed as if
he was trying to control conflicting emotions. Even
with his practised deception, his uncertainty showed in
the depths of his haunted eyes. 'Don't ask.'

'I am! What do you know?' she demanded huskily.
'Are you trying to hide something? You do know
things about my father, don't you?' she cried, waiting
for his reply in an agony of suspense.

'It would seem that he wanted to conceal his past,'
he said, as if grudging her that information. He studied
his hand-made shoes thoughtfully.

She shook her head in bewilderment. 'But why? He
was a good man, Lucenzo. He adored his family——'

'Get out of Venice,' he grated. 'Leave well alone.
There may or may not be something here he wanted
to hide. You don't want to know about your father's
past. Keep his memory sweet.'

She quailed at his heartless words, afraid of discovering that her adored father had feet of clay but
determined to face the truth. 'It's too late,' she said
heavily. 'I must know the truth. I have to see if this
key fits the deposit box and if there's anything there
which will throw some light on my family.' She reached
inside the neck of her sweater and drew out the key
on its chain. 'It is my right,' she said defiantly. 'You
can't legally stop me. Take me to the vault.'

Judging by his fiercely clenched teeth beneath the
rigid golden jaw, he was ready to erupt. Innocent of
intrigue, Meredith suddenly discovered it in the dark
depths of Lucenzo Salviati's eyes. The mask stiffened.
The eyes lanced hers with swift rage and her pulses
raced. He was hiding something. A secret, which he
was determined not to share. And Meredith burned to
know what that secret was.

Down a flight of elegant steps, flanked by a marble
balustrade, lay the bank's medieval vaults, protected
by a series of barley-twist iron gates. Meredith shiv-

ered in the damp air, wondering how many merchants
had stored their riches here in the past. And their
secrets. Love letters, perhaps. She frowned. Not her
father. He'd loved her mother devotedly, and had
married at twenty—surely too young to have had a
past?

'It's like a prison,' she said warily, peering through
the final gate at the rows of lead-lined boxes let into
the mellow brick walls.

Lucenzo plunged the key into the lock and let the
creaking gate swing open. 'In you go.'

She looked at him uncertainly, unsure about his
bland invitation. There was a rather menacing set to
his mouth. 'You could shut me in there and no one
would know,' she said with a half-laugh to hide her
nervousness.

'I could,' he drawled.

A small tremor ran through her body. The boxes
inside the vault looked fascinating and she badly
wanted to know what lay inside box number forty-
seven, but not if it meant going into the sinister little
room on her own. Lucenzo owned the bank. He could
do what he liked in it.

'You must come too,' she said finally, her nerves
strung as tightly as bowstrings.

'I was planning to,' he said with a sardonic smile.

Meredith thought it was the smile of the cat who'd
found a whole vat of cream. She paused, then took
courage in both hands and walked in with deceptive
boldness.

'You pride yourself on your fearlessness,' commented Lucenzo.

'Surely I have nothing to fear?' she challenged.

'If you have, you'll find out soon enough,' he said
enigmatically.

Inwardly she trembled, but she managed to glare at
him and searched up and down the narrow aisles for
the right number. At the far end of the vault she found
it. For a long time, she just stood in front of the box,

petrified. Then she took a deep breath. There was no sense in prolonging the agony.

With trembling fingers she tried the lock. There was a harsh sound of rust grating against rust, which set Meredith's teeth on edge, but the key wouldn't budge. 'It's stuck!' she cried in dismay.

'Shame.' Lucenzo didn't sound sorry at all. 'Maybe it isn't one of our keys. You could try another bank.'

She threw him a quick glance. He was leaning casually against a nearby brick pillar, his dark eyes watching her carefully. He eased his broad shoulders away from it and strolled slowly towards her, a faint, confident smile playing about his lips.

Meredith shrank back, alarmed by the unpleasant intention behind his expression. Then common sense and anger got the better of her and she firmed her mouth and concentrated on gently trying to wriggle the key free.

'Allow me,' he purred. His big hand enclosed hers, ruthlessly prised her fingers from the key and insolently took possession of it. 'Let's try a little brute strength, shall we?' He conjured up a coaxing grin, his teeth a perfect and dazzling white in the darkness of his face.

She wasn't fooled. Her eyes hardened to blue ice. Lucenzo was smiling for a special reason, though she was darned if she knew why. 'Give me back my key!' she demanded.

'Men's work,' he said infuriatingly.

Outrage turned to agitation when she saw that he was jamming the key in the lock with such force that the flesh on his fingers was turning white. She looked in horror at his hand, and the small specks of rust which were staining his skin from where he was exerting such extreme pressure.

'Stop doing that!' She clutched his hand and he half shouldered her away impatiently. 'Don't! Please!' she wailed in exasperation. 'You'll snap the key! If it is the right one, I'll never be able to see what's inside!'

'I can feel it turning,' he claimed obstinately. 'Give it a moment.'

'No! Leave it at once!'

'Almost there,' he said grimly.

Meredith was amazed that he couldn't see that the old key would never stand up to the pressure he was putting on it. And then she realised that he actually meant to force the key to breaking-point.

Infuriated, she wriggled under his barricading arms, whirled around and pushed violently at his chest with all her might. He staggered, his back slamming against the wall across the aisle. The brief flash of frustrated fury in his eyes made her stop in astonishment.

'I'm sorry,' she said, appalled at what she'd done. 'But you made me——' She stopped. He wasn't even looking at her. His glance was fixed mesmerically on something behind her right ear.

'*Madonna*!' he breathed.

She spun on her heel and saw what had happened: the lead door had swung open—and inside, something was gleaming. 'Oh, it *was* the right key!' she cried excitedly, forgetting him immediately. 'How extraordinary! There's a model boat in there!'

'Interesting,' murmured Lucenzo. 'A fake gondola.'

'What do you mean "a fake gondola"?' Carefully she drew it out. For its size it was heavy, and she nearly dropped it, Lucenzo's hands quickly sweeping beneath hers and supporting them in a lightning reflex.

He took the boat from her and examined it. 'There was a spate of these flooding the market in the 1950s,' he said in an offhand tone. 'They sold to ignorant millionaires like hot cakes. They were made from painted lead.'

'It looks real enough to me,' frowned Meredith.

'It probably looked real enough to the millionaires, too,' he said sardonically. 'Are you aware that gold never alters, never loses its shine, even after years beneath the sea, or buried in the ground? Well, this is pink and green here.' He pointed to different sections which had discoloured almost in a wavy pattern.

'A fake. Pity,' she said, stroking the smooth silken finish. It had been painted well. 'Is it worth much?'

He gave an elaborate shrug of his shoulders. 'People might be interested for its curiosity value.'

Her head bent over the exquisite gondola. 'It's beautifully made.'

Lucenzo's mouth quirked. 'By a master.' He placed the gondola carefully on a small ledge to one side of the deposit box.

Her eyes flicked to his. 'My. . .my father?'

'Was he good with his hands?'

She gave a rueful laugh. 'No. Terrible.'

'Then it's nothing to do with you after all.' He went to close the box but she grabbed his arm.

'Don't do that. I can see something else.' Meredith stretched into the depths of the box and removed a Venetian mask, moulded into the shape of a face. Its satin ribbons were worn and the gold paint was flaking, but it must have been lovely once with its tear-drop pearls artfully placed on the cheek. 'What odd things to put in a deposit box!' she said, intrigued, putting it beside the gondola.

'Eccentric,' agreed Lucenzo. 'Right, well, I suggest we put these back and close the box. They obviously don't mean anything to you, so it looks increasingly as if this whole business must have been a dreadful mistake. Perhaps your father got hold of the wrong key.'

He stretched across her once more to shut the lead door, his arm in front of her face and blocking her view of the box. But she'd seen something else, something white, like a document, and her hopes rose.

'Move aside,' she commanded sharply. She held her breath, wondering if he would defy her, and for a long moment their eyes locked in battle. Yet when he lowered his arm Meredith had the odd sensation that she'd lost. She foraged deeper inside the box with her arm plunged in almost up to the shoulder.

'These boxes were designed for bags of gold in the Middle Ages. And for people with longer arms than you. Let me get it.' Lucenzo's husky voice behind her sounded in her ear, his face so close that his breath flowed softly over her cheek, making her knees weaken.

Fatally, she twisted her head to one side and looked back at him. 'I've almost. . .got. . .it,' she jerked shakily, unable to tear her eyes from his. For they were melting as she stood there, and she seemed to be liquid inside too, her limbs strangely turning to water.

She felt his hands on her waist, pulling her ruthlessly away from the box so that she was forced to withdraw her hand. And he was turning her around, hauling her close to him in a quick, masterful movement.

'Oh, yes, you've got it,' he whispered. 'Enough to make me lose control of myself.'

Before she could jerk herself out of her shocked paralysis, he had angled his head and driven his ruthless, demanding lips down to collide with hers in an explosion of sensation. Meredith pulled back in alarm, but his hand slid up her spine to cradle her head, immobilising it and making her an easy prey. Angrily he crushed her mouth harder against his as he plundered her lips with a ferocity that took her breath away.

It was almost as if by kissing her he released some of that pent-up fury which lay simmering inside him. His kisses weren't gentle. They ground into her soft lips brutally, his hands, his body as hard as iron and totally merciless.

Small moans of protest sounded in her throat but they seemed to excite him more, because he growled with satisfaction, his lips branding hers with heat. And slowly that heat found an answer in her wakening body, Lucenzo's expert, demanding and ferocious kisses a world away from the enthusiastic but unexciting lunges from the young men at home.

They had asked. He took. And for some reason it was what she wanted. She shuddered with mortification.

His hands stroked her body in sensual caresses, arousing her unfairly, and she desperately wanted to lean into his vital, masculine strength and inhale the fresh scent of his skin and feel its smooth perfection. But she dared not.

'Let me go!' she cried huskily, as his lips began a tour of her throat.

'Meredith,' he crooned in his gravelly voice. 'You are quite the most tantalising——'

'I'm not! You know I'm not!' she cried hotly, pushing at his shoulders with all her might. 'You're making fun of me——'

Her words were enveloped by his swooping mouth again, covering hers. But this time she staggered back at the force of his tongue, invading, probing and making her gasp with unwanted pleasure. No man had kissed her like that. The sensation rocked through her, and she wanted only to remain there, feeling the suggestive thrust of his tongue as it explored the inner softness of her mouth and gently, expertly made her intensely and inescapably aware of the hard, pulsing heat of his virile manhood pressing insistently against her thighs.

'God, Meredith! You're driving me crazy with wanting. Let's get out of here,' he husked, flicking his tongue around the high, throbbing curve of her lips.

Her heavy lids lifted and she stared at him, bewildered, stunned by her own inexplicable reaction. She actually wanted him to take her somewhere and. . . She blushed furiously, then moaned as his finger found the centre of one breast and a million sparks flew to every corner of her body.

'No,' she groaned, clutching ineffectually at his strong hand. 'I—I—please, Lucenzo! Don't do that!'

Her huge blue eyes pleaded with him and then darkened at the flagrant desire in his expression.

'This enthusiastic response from your body isn't innocence,' he said in quiet triumph. 'Your eyes tell me exactly what you need. Don't waste time by playing games. I want you, Meredith. I want to take you away somewhere quiet and private and touch every inch of your naked body——'

'No!' she cried in horror. 'I'm not—I——'

His palm was rotating over her breast, filling her with a delicious lassitude, the unfamiliar feeling overwhelming her in the way that it took over her whole body, his touch vibrating through every nerve and firing every pulse. She let her lashes flutter down briefly to shut out the sight of Lucenzo's smouldering eyes, which seemed to be mesmerising her into surrender. A small moan whispered from her swollen mouth.

'That's right,' he coaxed in a satin-smooth voice, his hands exploring with such delicacy that her treacherous body strained for his touch. 'Give in to your senses. Let's go upstairs to the *salotto* and make love——'

Suddenly she released all the tenseness from her muscles, he relaxed his hold slightly, a surprised expression on his face that she should capitulate so easily, and she lifted her head with cold pride in every line of her body.

'Lucenzo Salviati, you are acting dishonourably. Would you take what doesn't belong to you? I'm not used to the clever, practised attentions of men like you. You're stronger than I am, and I know you could make me do. . .' she lowered her lashes in embarrassment '. . .things. . .that I don't want to do. What will that make you? Where is your pride? Leave me alone. Other women will be more willing.'

Her tiny figure shook with new-found sensations and her hands lifted in an involuntary gesture to touch her tingling breasts. A crimson stain swept up her face when she felt how swollen her breasts were, and how hard the crests were pressing against each hot palm. Her body belonged to someone else, she thought miserably, not her. It had a life of its own.

'You are very eloquent on behalf of your honour——'

'My virginity is more important to me than an hour or two of easily forgotten pleasure,' she broke in. 'I know I'm old-fashioned. That's how I was brought up—to value my body.'

Lucenzo looked extraordinarily white. 'For God's sake, Meredith, get out quickly!' he growled. '*Run!* Before——'

'I never run from anyone,' she ground out.

His eyes narrowed and flicked briefly to the open box behind her, and suddenly, with an appalling cramping of her stomach, Meredith knew that his glance had betrayed his true purpose in pretending to want her and making her flee from the vault without properly investigating its secrets.

'You swine!' she cried. 'You've been trying to divert my attention from the box! You devious, underhand, ruthless swine!'

Quick as a flash, she lunged inside the box for the sheet of paper which she'd seen there. In silence she scanned it rapidly. Her face drained of colour. At last she knew what he'd been keeping from her. And she almost wished she *had* run away.

CHAPTER FIVE

'Don't keep it to yourself,' said Lucenzo tightly.

He seemed as tense as she was, his whole body wound up like a coiled spring. Too shocked, too intensely angry to speak, she contemptuously passed the document to him with a hand that shook so much that he steadied it with his, an expression close to pity on his face as he carefully extracted the paper from her numb fingers. There was a long silence while he read. And then he lifted his head and his face was quite impassive.

'Meredith——' he began.

'Don't *speak* to me!' she croaked hoarsely. Violently she shook off his outstretched hand, and the English document announcing her father's change of name fluttered to the ground. 'Don't *touch* me!' Her voice broke and she stared blindly ahead. 'Father was Italian,' she whispered.

'Venetian,' corrected Lucenzo grimly.

She felt hysterical. 'What does it matter?'

'To a Venetian, it matters,' he said softly.

'You quibble about names, and I've just discovered that my father was once called Antonio Corosini!' she cried bitterly. 'Corosini!' Her stomach somersaulted. The implications began to whirl around her head, and she gave a little groan. 'The blackmail,' she said weakly. 'Oh, dear heaven! I can't bear this!'

'You have no choice. You brought this on yourself.'

At his uncompromising, pitiless remark, she covered her face with her hands, wanting to shut out Lucenzo's cruel eyes. Tears welled up in her eyes, and she did nothing to stop them from spilling through her fingers and on to her cheeks. Her father had a past which he'd taken pains to cover up. Perhaps a murky one—

90

otherwise why would he bother? And he had lied, she thought miserably. They had all lied to her.

'The whole of my life. . .' she rasped. 'It's been built on a cover-up. No wonder there were no photographs of his past. No wonder he clammed up whenever I asked him about his childhood. How could he do this to me?' she said, her voice trembling with emotion.

'Perhaps he wanted to protect you,' said Lucenzo gruffly.

'From what?' she asked, her eyes enormous as they shot open. Her wet lashes blinked furiously as Lucenzo scowled down on her tear-streaked face. 'What else didn't they tell me?'

She sobbed in the absolute silence of the cold vault. Lucenzo made no attempt to comfort her. It was as if he had turned into a block of ice. Overwhelmed by the devastating revelation, she sank to the floor, crying jerkily while Lucenzo watched imperviously, not moving a single muscle. He was as cold as the stone she sat on, she thought forlornly. Any normal man would comfort someone in her situation.

And suddenly, without warning, Meredith's slow temper flared into flames, fanned by Lucenzo's apparent indifference and the shameful memory of her sexual awakening beneath his marauding hands.

'My *father*!' she yelled. 'You knew all the time, didn't you, that he was Venetian?'

'Yes.'

The bold, brutal answer was like a douche of icy water. 'How *could* you? You shouldn't have tried to conceal the truth from me. I had a right to know, a right!'

In her rage, she leapt up and pummelled at his unresisting chest, hot tears flowing down her flushed cheeks till his cold, emotionless face was a blur. After a while she realised she'd been beating at him with her fists hard enough to hurt and yet he hadn't lifted a finger to stop her. A little ashamed of losing her self-

control so completely, she dashed a hand across her
eyes and glared up at him.

'Carry on. Hit me if you have to. Don't mind my
feelings,' he said in a throaty growl, his long, thick
lashes concealing the expression in his eyes.

'Oh! You inhuman monster! You're mocking me!'
she cried. 'You're totally cold-blooded and unfeeling!
How can you stay detached when my life is disinte-
grating? You could have prepared me for this——'

'No,' he said abruptly. 'I might have suspected, but
only key-holders know what is in their boxes.'

'Corosini didn't know?' demanded Meredith.
Lucenzo shook his head emphatically. 'But you were
aware that he and Father were related, weren't you?'
she persisted doggedly.

'Yes.'

Meredith's breath shuddered out at his admission,
her face distorted with pain. 'Now I understand!' she
said slowly. 'This was what Gran must have been
trying to tell me, poor darling. No wonder she was
distraught! She wanted me to know about Father.' She
groaned and her head tipped back. It must have been
terrible for her gran, wanting to explain about the
Italian connection, and being unable to.

'Meredith,' said Lucenzo in a steely tone. 'Don't
pursue this. It could change your life.'

Her head snapped back down in a flurry of bouncing
coppery hair, her eyes warily searching Lucenzo's face
for some sign of compassion. And there was none. 'It
has changed it! I'm not the same person who walked
in here. I'm half-Italian, for a start. I belong to a
family I know nothing about and I don't feel secure or
grounded any longer. Just what are you warning me
about?' she asked hoarsely. 'More skeletons in my
cupboard? Is the Corosini family something to be
ashamed of?'

'*No!*' cried Lucenzo savagely.

She flinched. 'Well, something other than sex gets

you aroused to a passion,' she said with unaccustomed acidity.

A blaze of anger flashed across his face and was quickly suppressed. 'Pretend it never happened. Keep what memories you have intact,' he muttered.

'No. They're shattered now,' she cried fervently. 'Don't you see? Any thought of turning my back on all this is impossible now. For pity's sake, help me! This is the most important thing that's ever happened to me in my life——'

'Oh, sure,' he snarled. 'Think of the money you can make! That's what it boils down to, isn't it?' he grated savagely. 'Your grandmother screwed cash out of Corosini for ten years. Her behaviour might have been questionable, but that money is now yours. You can keep every single penny for your tawdry little ambitions——'

'Stop this!' she exploded, surprising herself with the violence of her emotions.

She'd always had a passionate side to her nature, she thought, suddenly making sense of her reactions to life. Everyone had said how Welsh that was. It was also *Italian*. Venetian. Her eyes scanned Lucenzo's. They came from the same country. The struggle to understand everything showed clearly on her face, and slowly, surely, she found a ray of hope in the mess, something to compensate for the painful discovery that she'd been ignorant of her own roots.

She had a family. Here, in Venice! She smiled shakily, hopefully, through her tears.

'Oh, here it comes. A change of approach,' said Lucenzo cynically. 'The sweet smile gets turned on! Damn you, Meredith!' he seethed. 'You will not coax me into an indiscretion, so save your breath.'

With an effort, she reined back her impatience. He knew a great deal about her family and he was very important to her. 'Lucenzo, I know you're being loyal to your client, and I can admire that——'

'Spare me the sugar.'

'You have no reason to be so suspicious of me,' she said quietly.

He grunted. 'Don't I?'

'I'm used to people calling a spade a spade, and I don't understand sophisticated people,' she said quietly. 'But I do know when I'm being railroaded. You want the best for your client. So do I. He's a relative of mine.' Her face glowed. 'A living relative.' She smiled gently.

'He wants you to leave him alone.'

'But that's because he doesn't know me,' she said calmly. 'Nor does he know my intentions.'

Lucenzo tensed, his eyes glowering dangerously as if to threaten her. 'And they are?'

'To unite the family again. Families shouldn't be at loggerheads.' She saw his quick frown and hastened to explain. 'Look, I don't care a scrap about the money, I've told you that before. I'll return every penny. You see, I've found something far more valuable.'

His eyes flickered down to the gondola. 'Like what?' he asked harshly.

She clasped her hands in excitement, every inch of her suffused with an irrepressible happiness. 'Everything I've always wanted,' she answered gently, her warm smile lighting her whole face. Lucenzo looked unconvinced, but she persevered. 'Can't you understand? My dream has come true!'

'I bet,' he said scathingly.

'My goodness, I hope I never become as cynical as you,' she sighed. He winced. 'I'm not ashamed to be excited at the discovery that I have relatives in this world after all. *That's* what I've been wanting, every second of every day. I yearn for the love and affection I once had,' she cried passionately. 'Somewhere out there are people who may or may not know of my existence, people I can call my own——'

'Or people you'd wish you'd never met,' he said softly.

Meredith's delight was jolted by his remark. 'What are you trying to tell me?'

His eyes brooded on her, and it was a moment or two before he spoke. 'Why do you think your father left them in the first place?'

'I—I don't know!' Her impatient dismissal of his remark changed as she began to think more clearly. 'Maybe there was a row,' she frowned. 'You tell me.'

Lucenzo reached out and pushed back the tress of copper hair which had fallen over her forehead, and she trembled at the sensual drift of his fingers over her face. 'Meredith,' he said quietly, his voice as soft as silk, 'your father ordered that his possessions should be burnt. Everything that identified his background was destroyed. Doesn't that tell you something?'

'Yes. That it was a really serious quarrel,' she muttered unwillingly, shutting her mind to his line of reasoning. She didn't want her reunion with her family to be spoilt. Lucenzo was doing his best to put her off, and she resented his interference.

'Or that he didn't want to face up to certain consequences,' said Lucenzo brutally.

Her eyes widened. 'Are you suggesting he was on the run?'

He nodded, his mouth sharply sculpted in disapproval. 'On the run from *something*, wouldn't you say?' he drawled.

'No! Father was a darling. I want to be part of this family. I'm going to find them, and nothing you say is going to stop me. The quarrel is all in the past, and I'll heal any wounds. I can move mountains,' she finished, setting her stubborn mouth.

Her chin was tipped up by a ruthless finger. 'Meredith,' he drawled, 'you're full of surprises.' His wicked, mocking eyes gleamed down at her. 'But you can't go against your father's wishes. He never wanted you to meet your Venetian relatives.'

Her pale face lifted to his. 'I feel I've opened

Pandora's box,' she mumbled, remembering the old legend.

'It's an appropriate comparison. You've let out a bag of trouble for yourself,' said Lucenzo harshly.

'And hope,' she said truculently, recalling what had been left in Pandora's box.

'You're so damn determined to see the bright side! Your father was in serious trouble. For what other reason would he deny his birthplace? No one in his right mind would leave this city unless forced.'

She slumped against the wall, all the energy drained from her. 'A crime, you mean? Oh! The forgeries of the gondolas!' she hazarded. 'He was involved——'

'Who knows?' grunted Lucenzo.

Emotions tussled within her. Was this what Lucenzo *knew* for a fact, or was he trying to put her off—on the instructions of his client? Her face fell with disappointment.

'I wanted to be part of a family again,' she said dully. 'I saw myself sitting around a huge table eating supper with an assortment of generations—the way they do in all the films I've seen about Italians.'

'You mean like *The Godfather*?' he murmured.

She blinked and clutched at the wall behind her for support, searching his bland, secretive face to see if that was a blatant threat. But he held all the keys to the boxes she wanted to unlock, and, however suspicious, however wary she was of him, she had to persuade him to help her.

'Lucenzo,' she said soberly, making a direct appeal to him, 'you love your family, don't you? Your own flesh and blood?'

His white teeth bit into his lower lip, and he appeared to be considering his reply. 'I was adopted.'

She looked at him in astonished silence and went bright red with embarrassment, remembering what she'd said previously about adopting children. 'Oh, I am sorry,' she said huskily. 'Forgive me—it's a sensitive area. I was very thoughtless in what I said earlier. But you are devoted to your family nevertheless, aren't you?'

'Yes.' He seemed distant, as if thinking of them. 'You say you can move mountains. I build them, for the woman who adopted me,' he said, half under his breath.

There was no doubting his passion. She relaxed a little. 'Lucenzo, I beg you, please talk to Corosini. He's my kinsman,' she pleaded. 'You're in his confidence, aren't you? Persuade him to see me. The last thing I want is to upset him or the family—I can't bear hurting people—but I'm harmless; you can tell him that!'

'Can I?' he muttered. 'Are you?' He regarded her sourly. 'It seems to me that you're more dangerous than a jungle full of tigers.'

She caught his arm urgently. 'That's ridiculous!' she cried impatiently. 'A meeting. I ask for nothing more. You can't deny me.'

'I can't betray the Corosini,' said Lucenzo stiffly. 'I'm supposed to keep you apart.'

'Then if you were acting on orders and through a sense of misguided loyalty, I forgive you,' she said generously, and was rewarded by his amazed laugh.

'Please, Meredith,' he said faintly. 'I can't take any more of your good nature. You're breaking me on the rack of your virtue.'

'It does have its own rewards, then,' she smiled.

'Apparently so,' he said slowly, tension beginning to ease from his body at last.

'I know things will turn out all right. You will help me?' she said persuasively, turning the full power of her bright blue eyes on him.

He looked at her for several interminable seconds. 'It means that much to you?' She nodded. His shoulders lifted and fell in a huge exhalation of breath. '*Allora*. How can I fight sincerity?' he muttered, but, to Meredith's joy, was obviously wavering. Her eyes

sparkled like sunlit water. 'Hell,' he said grudgingly.
'I'll think about it.'

'Wonderful! Oh, you won't regret it——'

'I think I will,' he said wryly.

'No. You and Corosini will be happy, I promise.
Thank you, thank you!' she cried, quite ecstatic that
he'd unbent.

'I only said I'd *think* about it, Meredith,' he said,
sounding bemused. 'Your innocence would disarm the
devil himself.'

She laughed delightedly, too happy to care about
anything but the fact that her trip had brought her an
undreamed-of surprise. Whatever the trouble, it was
in the past. She knew he would give in eventually.

'Well, that takes care of you,' she said cheekily.
'What about Corosini?'

Lucenzo's eyes were veiled. 'You could disarm him
too,' he conceded.

'I could hug you!' she cried in glee.

'I don't think that would be very wise,' he murmured. 'I think I could do with several cups of strong
black coffee. We'll go to the Piazza,' he said decisively.
'Bring the gondola and the mask.'

She smiled. 'Oh, yes! At last I have something of
Father's. Could you find me a carrier bag?' she asked.
'This mask is shedding paint like mad.' As she lifted it
out, a piece of flaking gold paper floated to the floor
and, to her astonishment, Lucenzo picked the little
piece up with finger and thumb.

He saw her look and gave a small shrug. 'Habit,' he
said. 'Tidy mind.'

But she hardly heard him. Her mind was whirling,
preoccupied with her own thoughts. Lucenzo was her
one link with her father's family—that and the name,
of course. Corosini. Meredith Corosini. She smiled
wistfully. Who were they? What did they do? And,
she wondered anxiously, had her noble-looking father
really done something dishonest?

Instead of solving a mystery, she'd discovered

another. She dearly wanted to see her family and persuade them to forget the ill-feeling that had split the Corosini apart. She would work on Lucenzo and coax an address from him.

Blissfully happy, she walked with Lucenzo through the crowded, music-filled streets of Venice, feeling familiar already with the funny little tunnels, the magnificent churches and pretty *campos*. They were now part of her heritage, and she looked on them with freshly delighted eyes.

They came to a lurching pontoon, where she clung to him in excitement, her eyes enormous at the sight of four enormous man-sized earwigs calmly waiting for the ferryboat. They were chatting beneath coloured umbrellas, their giant pincers waggling as they gestured.

'Lucenzo!' she whispered in admiration. 'I've never seen such incredible costumes! How do you think they get those pincers to stay up? It's a miracle of engineering.'

'This isn't any old carnival, Meredith. It's simply the best in the world. People spend six months making their costumes. These are good, but you'll see even better ones in the Piazza.'

'I make costumes myself,' she told him eagerly, eyeing up and down a Harlequin who'd appeared beside her. The stitching of the seams was particularly fine. Harlequin laughed at her fascination, and she laughed back happily.

'You told me you work with children,' frowned Lucenzo.

'I do. The crèche I run is in a factory. The children's parents help me to put on pantomines to raise money for outings and the Christmas party.'

'I might have guessed,' he muttered drily. 'Any other worthy good deeds you'd like to mention?'

'I organise the jumble sales for Oxfam and the annual pig-roast for Help The Aged. . . Oh, and I do

the monthly teas for the Valley Choir,' she said,
thinking of them fondly.

His eyebrow lifted, and Meredith realised he was
paying her close attention. 'I'm impressed. You must
be a good organiser.'

'I'm practical. I get on and do things while other
people are talking about them,' she said without an
ounce of boastfulness. 'The choir teas take it out of
me, though.' She laughed ruefully. 'One hundred
hungry men! I'm baking for the whole week before-
hand! But it's very satisfying.' She grinned cheekily.
'You sound as if you're interviewing me for a job.'

Lucenzo frowned. With a roar of its engine, the
ferry rode into the landing stage with a heavy thud,
throwing Meredith against Lucenzo. They both gasped
as the breath was knocked out of them by the impact.
Her mouth was within an inch of his chin and they
clung to one another for a heart-stopping moment,
getting breath and balance back, before he thrust her
aside.

'Sorry,' he said curtly. 'Did I hurt you?'

'It's all right,' she grinned, too happy to mind. 'It's
OK, we're not related,' she joked. His mouth thinned.
'Forgive me for being flippant,' she sighed. 'I just feel
like leaping around and celebrating, I'm so happy!
Once I've met everyone and we've had a chance to get
to know one another, they'll see no reason to continue
this quarrel.'

He gave an ironic laugh. 'You make it seem so
simple.'

'It is, I promise you.'

Her radiant smile seemed to melt his icy mask.
Gradually, reluctantly, his own lips curved, and then
his eyes joined in, twinkling like glimmering black
pools. And she had to drag her gaze away because she
began to drown.

The journey down the Grand Canal was a magical
one for Meredith, in her warm glow of contentment.
The snow was coming down in thick flakes, adding to

the unreal appearance as they chugged slowly from one bank to the other, and she was delighted that they stopped at every single stop. Her nose was pressed permanently against the window of the boat in an effort to see every beautiful palace with its sleek black gondolas bobbing against the striped poles at the end of jetties, waiting for some prince or wealthy politician to step into.

And everywhere she looked were quite dazzling costumes: foxes being ferried across in the stand-up *traghettos*, Mozart look-alikes, women in huge pannier skirts negotiating the gap between jetties and throbbing motor-launches.

'How could my father leave?' she breathed, her face shining. 'This is heavenly.'

Conflicting emotions played across Lucenzo's face, and he wrenched his eyes from hers to contemplate the view. 'Look,' he said gruffly. 'Santa Maria della Salute.' The words sounded like a phrase of love, the way he said them. Touched, she turned her attention to where he was pointing. 'We get off the stop after Salute,' he said warmly, as if pleased at her awed silence as she took in the building's perfection. 'Since you haven't done any of the tourist sights, I'll take you past the Palazzo Ducale—the Doges' Palace—into the Piazza San Marco.'

The crowds were tremendous. Meredith was glad of Lucenzo's arm around her waist—essential if she was to stay near him. They were jostled and pushed, and all the while she was catching glimpses of stunning costumes. To her amusement, two black-cloaked figures in full face masks and tricorn hats detached themselves from a group on a parapet and arranged themselves in exaggerated attitudes of extreme sorrow, one studying a rose, the other a silver mirror.

'Who are these people?' she giggled, impressed by the melodrama. 'Actors?'

He glanced briefly at her amused face and shrugged. '*Non lo so*. I don't know. That's the point of the disguises. Waiters, lawyers, princes, paupers—who knows? Carnival gives the poor a chance to mingle with the rich. If they stay silent, their dialects will never give them away and they can be whoever they like.'

'What fun!' she said with a laugh. 'That must appeal to your sense of intrigue.'

'Of course. At Carnival time nothing is ever what it seems.'

'In Venice, at any time, nothing is ever what it seems,' she said drily.

'The innocent becomes a sceptic,' he drawled. 'Don't change, Meredith. There are too many cynics in this world without you joining them. We must talk. The cheaper *caffès* will be packed. Why don't we splash out and go into Florian's? We can wear masks and no one will know who we are.'

'I know waiters,' she said. 'They can spot a fake at twenty paces. They'll take one look at my clothes and know I'm as poor as a church mouse.'

'I'll buy you an expensive mask and confuse them,' he suggested.

While Lucenzo looked through the displays on a gaily decked stall, Meredith gently extracted her father's gold mask from the tissue in which he'd carefully wrapped it. Lifting it to her face, she discovered that it was lined in fine padded silk. It covered the whole of her face, shaping to its contours and jutting out with an exaggerated jawline.

She was trying the black velvet ribbons behind her head when Lucenzo's hand descended on one wrist violently. 'Take that off!' he husked in strangled tones.

'Why?' she protested, her voice muffled. 'I feel different. Ow! Lucenzo, you're crushing my bones!'

'If you wear that,' he said curtly, 'you'll destroy one of the few things your father possessed. It's fragile. Keep it wrapped up. Wear this.' His relentless grip increased till she was forced to let go of the ribbon.

He removed the mask and covered her face with a bright turquoise sequinned one he'd chosen for her.

'You're right. Thanks. You can be really thoughtful sometimes,' she said gratefully, puzzled by his sharp hiss of exasperation.

'Beautiful. Stunning,' he growled in a low, dangerously seductive voice, tying the new mask firmly.

She blinked uncertainly at him, then laughed, realising what he'd meant. 'Thanks,' she said drily. 'The minute I cover my face, I'm beautiful?'

He slipped on a black velvet mask, only his golden hair and smouldering dark eyes betraying his identity. 'No. You're beautiful whatever you do to yourself,' he murmured, but she couldn't see his expression, and that was infuriating.

'You're a dreadful flirt,' she rebuked with a sigh. 'Quite a Casanova.'

'Poor man. He was imprisoned up there, beneath the lead roof,' Lucenzo said, pulling her close, his head against hers as she craned her neck to look at the pink and white Doges' Palace.

'I bet *he* sighed on that journey from the court to the prison, over the Bridge of Sighs,' she smiled.

'He had the right idea about women,' Lucenzo said cynically. 'He enjoyed them. Nothing more complicated than that.'

'Women have let you down,' she said sympathetically. 'One day you'll meet someone you want to share your life with. Marriage isn't a prison——'

'It would be for me,' he said quietly. 'I have too much to achieve, too few hours in the day to spend on keeping a wife happy. My wife would need all the virtues in the world to cope with the demands of my life. Stamina, poise, wisdom, dedication, a love of people from all walks of life——'

'Heavens! Do you have a part-time job I don't know about?' she grinned. 'Prince of Venice, for instance?'

'Come,' he said abruptly. 'I need that coffee.'

Meredith was fascinated by the brief glimpse into

his background, and wanted to ask why he needed to marry such a paragon. Then she remembered the way he'd looked when she'd talked about the Venetian nobility.

'Lucenzo——' Her hand was grabbed and she was being dragged along behind him as he shouldered his way through a group clustered around a hilarious puppet-show.

She was left thinking how hard he was driving himself for the sake of his adoptive family. Perhaps he felt he owed them something; to make a glittering society match for instance—whereas, she sighed, they would probably be perfectly happy with his company instead.

'Piazza San Marco,' announced Lucenzo, raising his voice above the sound of horns and bells. Multi-coloured streamers descended on their heads, making Meredith laugh until he saw fit to drape them gently over her hair, his face far too close. 'Napoleon,' he murmured, 'called this the finest drawing-room in Europe.'

'The builders forgot the roof,' she husked.

He smiled, as if knowing why she'd attempted a joke, and turned her around, leaning her into his body. '*Ecco*, Venice,' he said softly. 'Yours, mine. The essence of our love of grandeur, our flamboyance, our passion for self-expression. Does this daunt you or delight you?'

She looked around the vast square. Thronged with thousands of people, it was decorated with coloured lights and banners—and contained a huge striped circus tent. Three sides of the Piazza were bordered by arched colonnades, tiers upon tiers of them, like a massive wedding cake. Around her the crowd ebbed and flowed in a flurry of noise and colour, and Lucenzo's arm curled around her body as if he cared for her safety.

'I'm speechless!' she breathed.

'Pity. I like your chatter.'

She looked back at him in surprise and saw he meant that. A gentle smile spread over her face, unnoticed beneath her mask. Lucenzo was softening, hour by hour, the longer she was with him and the more she helped him to forget his relentless ambition and that intriguing private agony which had carved his face into such severe lines. She wanted to reach out and touch him, to tell him that life could be wonderful. Instead she said something banal.

'I feel proud that my father came from this city,' she said slowly. 'And I envy you for living here in these surroundings.'

'If it was good enough for Marco Polo, it's good enough for me.' Lucenzo gave her waist a little squeeze, and a pleasant glow warmed her. He was really letting go at last, she thought happily.

She loved the feel of his arm around her. She wanted to prolong the contact. 'Do you mind the tourists?' she asked.

'What would we do without them? The most famous painters, musicians and writers chose to live and work in Venice above all other cities. Tourists come to see the Titian ceilings, to hear Vivaldi, to see where Byron lived——'

'And Hemingway's bar,' put in Meredith.

Lucenzo laughed, his breath fanning her hair over her face. 'That too.'

'I want to stay,' she said, whirling around to confront him. 'There's so much to discover.'

His hands jerked her to him again as a group of jugglers pushed past, their clubs digging into her back so that she was forced to catch Lucenzo's shoulders and lean hard against him, totally at his mercy. She felt his fingers splayed across her back and stared up at his dark, aggressively sexy eyes.

'You could be easily hurt,' he said huskily, a note of warning in his voice.

'If anyone tries,' she said steadily, very conscious of the steel strength of his hands, 'they'll find that I have

a highly developed sense of self-preservation. I'm not
a coward; I don't flinch from facing trouble. I'm my
own woman, Lucenzo, so don't you or Corosini ever
forget that.'

His eyes melted into hers. 'I won't,' he said.

Meredith quivered, aware that the warmth of his
disarming smile was reaching into her own body, and
she was relieved when he released her. Fortunately
her mask disguised her emotions.

She turned her attention to what was happening all
around them, the laughter, the gossip, the spontaneous
singing of a Rossini aria. People were dancing everywhere, some in costume, some wrapped warmly
against the cold.

Flames and smoke from nearby chestnut-sellers and
the bare-chested fire-eaters flickered and drifted into
the dark grey sky, and Meredith just hung on to
Lucenzo, lost for words, overwhelmed by the volume
of sound, the bustle, the glamour, as they walked
along beneath the arched walkway of the Procuratie
Nuove.

'This is the Piazza as it should be,' Lucenzo mused,
'filled with people in period costume. I love Venice at
Carnival time. Look, over there.'

Six satin-cloaked figures in white porcelain masks
arranged themselves artistically against the façade of a
shop selling Murano glass, the blank stares and the
perfectly carved mouths giving them a look of
unreality. They all lifted their arms in unison, and a
battery of flashlights went off, making the jewel-like
colours of each robe shimmer as vibrantly as the vivid
hues of the glass in the shop window.

'I don't understand *why* they pose for the tourists,'
she said, marvelling at how the huge hoods were wired
to flare out in soft folds around each tightly wrapped
skull. 'Are they natural show-offs, or what?'

Lucenzo shook his head. 'Just people with dreams,
living a fantasy life while Carnival is on. You must try
it. It's really rather enjoyable to walk about incognito.'

'I'm always what I want to be,' she said with a frown. 'What about you? Do you pretend to be someone you're not?' She felt the muscles in the arm around her swell as he flexed them, and looked up at him, forgetting he was masked.

'I've worn costume at Carnival time,' he said smoothly, ducking the question.

'You ought to dress up as a Venetian noble,' she mused. 'You'd look fantastic in a wig and brocade jacket. You already stalk around like a haughty prince,' she teased.

'Looks can be deceptive,' he murmured.

A party of revellers in black and red velvet doublets and hose ran down the arcade, showering everyone with confetti. Laughing, she tossed back her hair with joy. 'Isn't it wonderful?' she cried. 'A whole city partying—*and* transported back into the eighteenth century!'

He looked with amusement at her small, vivacious figure almost bouncing alongside him with effervescent high spirits. 'I'm glad you're enjoying this,' he said huskily. There was a moment's hesitation. 'I certainly am. Let's eat a pile of sticky cakes in Florian's.'

Inside, a series of narrow rooms were filled with lounging aristocrats dressed in silks and satins ablaze with fake jewels. Meredith's mouth was open beneath her mask as Lucenzo imperiously led her to a favoured seat, followed by a posse of attentive waiters.

'You looked so regal, they didn't bother about me,' she whispered to him.

'Princely dignity comes naturally to a Venetian,' he said drily, removing his mask. A tray of coffee arrived almost immediately, together with an enormous plate of calorie-laden cakes. 'Florian's is famous. They've been serving coffee here for three hundred years,' he confided.

'My! No wonder the waiters looked tired,' she whispered.

Lucenzo grinned and held out a chocolate *tartuffe*.

Slowly she unlaced her mask too, not wanting to get it sticky, and submissively opened her mouth. All the time she was conscious of his eyes on her lips, her teeth, the way her mouth closed over the small cake, touching the tips of his fingers as it did so.

She drew back, pressing herself into the upholstered chair, and surreptitiously studied him in the gilt mirror opposite. There was something very sensual about the way he sat, apparently at ease, yet as aware of his own sexuality as she was.

'Tell me your favourite tune. We'll get the orchestra outside to play it,' he suggested.

'I have so many! I like "Memory",' she said hesitantly. 'I suppose you'll say that's corny, but I'm terribly sentimental.'

'Not at all. I've known women to choose something highbrow to impress me—and sit in an agony of boredom all the way through. I'm glad you don't try to be what you aren't,' he said gravely, beckoning the waiter who'd been leaning wearily against the door-jamb. Lucenzo made the request, and was about to place some notes in the man's hand when she stopped him, and both men looked at her askance.

'He's tired,' she said to Lucenzo gently. 'I'll go and ask.'

'And deprive the man of his tip?' he queried in astonishment.

'Oh. Well, tip him if you like, but I'll go in his place.'

Lucenzo coughed, covering his mouth and averting his head politely. The waiter's eyes had rounded and then slid to the now poker-faced Lucenzo, who became preoccupied with peeling the paper from a Carnival doughnut. 'The *signorina* is very kind to think of my aching legs,' bowed the waiter. 'However, I will be delighted to do this favour—free, from my heart.'

Meredith's warm smile made the two men respond with smiles of their own, then the waiter threaded his way out to the orchestra. 'You know,' she said to

Lucenzo, 'you don't have to keep waving money at people. I never do—I can't afford it. They'll do things gladly if you ask nicely enough.'

'But I don't think I quite have your astonishing nerve,' he said, laughing.

The poignant music drifted into the coffee-house, and Meredith settled back on the Victorian chair to enjoy it and her surroundings. Milling around outside were a few Cinderellas in ballgowns anxiously adjusting their wigs and checking their patches. A group of men leant on their gold-topped canes and talked to a pair of Ugly Sisters.

'Impressed with the glamour?' murmured Lucenzo, watching her intently.

'Of course I am! I haven't seen it before. I haven't seen *anything* like this before,' she said breathlessly. 'I'm living a fairy-tale,' she sighed happily. 'I'm going to be a princess——Ow!' she yelled, as Lucenzo's coffee spilled and splashed over her hand.

'Sorry. Clumsy of me. What were you saying?' he asked tightly, mopping at her hand with his monogrammed handkerchief.

She took it from him and patted the marble-topped table, then placed the hanky to dry over the back of a chair. 'I've forgotten; I got diverted. I don't know——'

'Princess?' he prompted.

'Oh, yes!' she grinned. 'On second thoughts, that's too permanent. I'm more like Cinderella, aren't I, having a couple of hours at a ball before she returns to the dishes?'

'I'm not Prince Charming,' he said drily.

'That's true. If you were three feet shorter, I might mistake you for Grumpy sometimes,' she ventured. His mobile mouth quivered. 'Oh, do smile and get it over with,' she urged, her eyes sparkling with triumph.

Quite startled, he roared with laughter, his face very relaxed and happy. 'You little witch,' he chuckled. 'How difficult it is to see you as an enemy.'

'I wish you wouldn't. I'm not. You've thawed,' she said contentedly. 'Like the snow on the Piazza.' The two bronze Moors on the clock-tower outside hammered on the bells to announce that it was midday. 'I feel. . .I feel as if I've been whisked away to another world,' she breathed, her face radiant.

'Would you like that?' he asked idly. 'You seem very happy in this setting.'

'I'm happy anywhere,' she said, enthusiastically tucking into a rum-flavoured cake. Her solemn eyes lifted to his. 'Places aren't important, only people. I'm especially happy if there are people I love around me. Even without your help I'd find my family,' she said in a low tone, 'and it wouldn't matter if I had to look up every Corosini in the phone book and knock on a hundred doors.'

There was a silence of several seconds while she held her breath. Lucenzo seemed to be making up his mind about her, and she knew intuitively that everything she longed for hung on his decision.

'Yes. You'd do that,' he said slowly. 'No one could ever accuse you of not persisting. It's an admirable trait. But you needn't go to all that effort,' he continued. 'Give me a little time, be patient, and trust me. It will take a while, I'm afraid, but I'll do everything I can to persuade the family that they should meet you.'

CHAPTER SIX

MEREDITH'S surroundings ceased to exist. She only saw Lucenzo's serious face and his dark, velvet black eyes. Then her hands began to shake so she put down the half-eaten cake, very aware that his face was full of emotion, belying the quietness of his voice. Trust him. Dared she?

'So I've passed the first hurdle,' she breathed.

He smiled enigmatically, and put his mask back on. 'I can't answer that question yet.'

She groaned. 'What do I have to do? Handstands?' she cried ruefully.

He lifted a roguish eyebrow. 'And bring the whole of Florian's to a grinding halt? Meredith. . .' He pushed his hand absently through his hair, leaving it dishevelled. She felt her heart contract. 'The situation is a little complicated——'

'No, it's not. You tried to stop me seeing my family,' she said with a frown. She turned aside, and, without thinking, pocketed the handkerchief. 'I might have given up——'

'Then you wouldn't have been tough enough to be a Corosini,' he replied evenly.

She grimaced. 'Good grief! Who are they, commandoes?'

'It seems like that sometimes. Shall we go outside and dance?'

Meredith was about to dig her heels in, but thought better of it. She had to stay on her best behaviour and dance to his tune. She gave a wry smile. She would dance. But, she thought mischievously, so would he, eventually. She'd get her own way.

The deceptively demure Meredith was led outside by the masked Lucenzo. He deftly turned her to face

him, and took her in his arms, drawing her close
because of the crowds. Violins were playing a Strauss
waltz, and he began to dance with her, making her
bend and sway to his direction, dominating every move
she made.

I'll remain passive, she thought meekly. Till I can
take control. But she found it impossible not to
respond—either to him, or to everything around them.
Meredith's senses were alerted to his hard, firm male
body, the command with which he manoeuvred them
around the square, the pressure of his fingers against
her supple spine.

Deliberately, she chattered and laughed, not trying
to contain her excitement. Gradually he grew less
remote as they spun around the Piazza, missing
nothing: the jesters, the acrobats, the medieval play
being performed in one corner, the drama students
creating masks with stage make-up, turning happy
faces into tearful Harlequins and nice-looking fathers
into wicked Satans. Nothing, she smiled to herself,
was what it seemed.

'*Permesso*?'

'Oh, it's Dandini!' she giggled.

'He wants to dance with you,' said Lucenzo. 'Go
on, Cinderella.'

Happily she drifted into the man's arms, and found
herself spinning from one partner to another, thrilled
with the magic of dancing in a snowy square, the
growing gloom lit by the dainty fairy lights and
lanterns.

'I thought I'd lost you,' said Lucenzo almost fondly,
when they found one another again after a long time.

'Heavens! Prince Charming again!' she cried
blithely. Meredith felt breathlessness claim her as his
possessive arms wrapped around her once more. It
was like being back with someone very special, she
thought in confusion. 'You nearly did lose me,' she
managed huskily. 'That last man—the one in the
Mozart wig without a mask—wanted to show me a

restaurant because I'm mad on cooking and drooled over the recipes he described.'

Lucenzo crushed her body closer to his, driving her into a fast, whirling quickstep, his thighs moving against hers with hard, male insistence. 'Mozart,' said Lucenzo drily, 'is a cantankerous old man who owns one of the best restaurants in Venice.'

'Really? I told him he looked like my milkman, and he laughed.'

'I imagine he would,' said Lucenzo wryly. 'No wonder he took to you. You're pretty good at getting on with people, aren't you? I watched you bring sunshine into the lives of each one of your partners.'

'You watched me?' she queried uncomfortably. It was a good thing she hadn't known or she would have been self-conscious. It worried her that he'd been secretly observing her. Why would he do that? 'Lucenzo. . .you're not leading me a dance, are you?' she asked, lifting her unhappy face to his.

He stopped in his tracks, gently swaying with her to the music. 'Meredith—I——' His confusion made her pulse race in alarm. He removed his mask, and she slowly loosened hers, staring into his eyes, trying to read what he hesitated to tell her.

'Cenzo! *Ciao*!' teased a low female voice.

His eyebrow lifted in ironic apology to Meredith, and he smiled benignly. '*Ciao*, Katarina.' Lucenzo kissed the stunning dark-ringleted Katarina warmly, three times on her cheeks. 'Excuse me a moment, Meredith,' he said, turning away.

Left alone, she admired Katarina's beautiful jewelled brocade dress beneath the heavy wool cape. Both items of clothing looked very expensive. She heard them begin to talk quietly in Italian, and she moved aside tactfully. And then he was seemingly swamped by women in period make-up and elegant costumes, some receiving an embrace on the lips from him, others obviously discontented when they received merely a light kiss on each cheek. A group of men in silks and satins joined the party, greeting Katarina as 'Contessa'. Meredith felt a spasm of pain in her breast.

Separated now from Lucenzo, she climbed the arcade steps close by and leant against a pillar, quietly observing his sophisticated friends, conscious of the gap between them and herself. He was a wealthy banker, urbane, sophisticated, charming. He moved in exalted circles—and was ambitious for greater things. And he held her future in his hands.

Up there on the top step, looking down on Lucenzo's bright fair head, she felt as if she stood on the brink of a great change in her life. He knew what that change would entail, and he wasn't sure she could handle it.

Her eyes roamed over the chattering women, all fawning over him, tossing their heads, slanting their eyes at him and laughing prettily. Only the beautiful Katarina remained relatively calm, her arm resting possessively on Lucenzo's shoulder as if she was totally confident of his interest. Only she, of all the women, seemed not to be competing for his attention.

Tongues of flame from a fire-eater near by lit Meredith's porcelain face with a golden glow and set her tumbling red waves ablaze on her shoulders. Lucenzo looked up as if he'd only just realised she'd slipped away, and seemed taken aback when he saw her. Like heat-seeking missiles, his eyes collided with hers and on his face was an unconcealed, raw, earthy hunger that made her clutch at the pillar for support.

She was aware of nothing else but his compelling, mesmeric eyes, which were rooting her to the spot, setting a torch to her, the shooting flames searing her insides. Heat flushed through her body, prickling over her skin and parching her throat, and she lifted a languid hand to push back her flowing hair.

'No!' she whispered, her mouth, her eyes denying what he intended.

'Yes,' he mouthed back.

Keeping his extraordinary savage eyes fixed on her,

he began to make his excuses and push the women
aside, forcing his way through the group towards her.
She stood as still as a statue, watching his determined
progress through the crush of people, while her heart
somersaulted in anticipation. Then he was looming
over her, inches away, and already the sexual hunger
in his body was enfolding her and the unreleased
tension within her was making her quiver from the top
of her head, down to her toes. And not one inch of
her was spared in between.

'I—I——' She blinked, her voice coming to a croaking halt.

He gave a slow smile. 'Lost your tongue?' he murmured huskily, totally in command of the situation.
'Been eating flames? Your throat is parched, your
mouth dry. . .' He licked his lips, contemplating her.

She shook her head in futile denial. Robbed of
speech, she tried to protest with her huge, bewildered
eyes. She felt herself being pulled into his body, then
his arms were wrapping around her.

'What. . .?' She froze, intensely aware of the powerful sinews in his thighs and the potential strength in
him. But worse, far worse, was his ability to render
her helpless whenever he touched her. She pleaded
with him silently.

'I know,' he muttered. 'This is the last thing I want
to happen now. But when I looked up and saw you,
all I could think of was holding you, kissing you——'

'Lucenzo!' she whispered in astonishment.

'I'm going to regret this, but I have to do it. I'm
driven. Forced.'

'F-forced? Who by?'

He gave her a look of savage need and then he was
kissing her fiercely. His lips hesitated, and she thought
for a moment that he was going to draw her away, but
he gave a low groan and his mouth moved against hers
again.

She hardly knew him. Yet they were now learning
to kiss as if they had been made for one another, she

thought in panic. 'Lucenzo. . .we shouldn't, we really shouldn't,' she managed, before he possessed her mouth again.

Gently. Expertly. The touch, the feel, the warmth of him was irresistible. Meredith kept herself as rigid as possible, but knew her whole body was singing with his. As his kiss deepened, his lips devoured hers with a sweetness that sent incredible curls of pleasure through the whole of her melting body.

'Perfection,' he muttered. 'I never imagined. . .' His mouth became occupied in tracing the line of her jaw.

She quivered, quite shaken by the erotic sensations the caress was arousing. 'Oh, no, no,' she moaned, helplessly lifting her hands to his hair.

Her denial wasn't spoken to stop him. It was to stop her. She was telling herself that she wasn't falling for him. The feelings she had were nothing to do with love, only a combination of. . . She shuddered, half leaning into his plundering mouth as it burned a fever into her throat. Her heavy eyes refused to stay open.

His hair was thick and warm, and her fingers revelled in the feel of it, creeping around the back of his skull where she half-heartedly tugged to bring his head back so that she no longer ached for his kisses to continue.

He deliberately surrounded her protesting mouth with his, the sculpted lips so persuasive that she felt every bone in her body weakening. Enclosed in darkness, in her own world of make-believe, she feebly allowed him to nuzzle her ear and then to kiss her thoroughly again, blissfully enjoying his skilled domination until she became nervously aware that he was sliding his hands beneath her coat and for a brief second of lancing flame he had cupped her breasts in his big, infinitely welcome hands.

'*No!*' she said forcibly, going against her own treacherous desire. Thrusting her palms angrily against his chest, she managed to bring them both back to earth again.

'You seem determined to drive me into the arms of easier women, Meredith.'

She winced, the force of his brutal remark piercing through her like a sharp knife, the suggestion of other women hurting so badly that she realised with a sick sensation that she was jealous.

'Time Cinderella left the party,' she said a little croakily. She tried hard to look composed, but it was more difficult than she could have imagined. Small but dangerously exciting trickles of pleasure were still winging their way through her virtually defenceless body. She gritted her teeth. 'I'm going to the tourist office right now, to see if there's anywhere I can stay tonight——' A sea of uplifted faces swam into her vision, and she coloured up with embarrassment. 'Oh,' she groaned. 'Your friends!'

His glance slid over to them, taking in the horrified Katarina surrounded by malicious-looking women. Meredith had the distinct impression that a hint of triumph had flashed in Lucenzo's eyes. 'Oh, dear!' he exclaimed, not sounding sorry at all. Nor, to Meredith's dismay, in the least surprised.

'What are you up to, Lucenzo?' she asked huskily.

'I'm in trouble. Fraternising with the——' He swore and clapped a hand to his forehead, but it was too late; the word didn't even need saying.

'The enemy?' supplied Meredith in a whisper, her face drained of colour. 'Oh, God! Is that how you still see me? What will my family think of me. . .?' She stopped, before her tears of humiliation broke through her weakened defences. She met that terrible barrier, his stony face, and glared at him angrily. 'Are you trying to destroy my reputation?'

'With a kiss?' he mocked.

'By parading me before your friends as a woman who'll let a virtual stranger kiss her passionately,' she said accusingly. 'My family won't want to know me! You rat! How dare you pretend to be attracted to me? Whose side are you on?' she asked hoarsely.

Lucenzo lowered his eyes. 'Ultimately the side that favours the future well-being of my family.'

Meredith looked at him with bitterness. He'd deceived and manipulated her again and again, and she'd fallen for it every time. His behaviour was unforgivable. 'Stop prevaricating!' she demanded. 'Answer me, Lucenzo! Answer me honestly for once, will you?' She watched him search helplessly for a reply, the hysteria rising within her that he might have ruined her chances of being accepted by her family.

'Honestly?' He frowned at her, playing for time.

'Yes!' she cried in exasperation. 'Don't you know the word? What are you trying to do to me?' she asked, a catch in her voice. 'You've made me feel cheap——'

'Cenzo!' scolded Katarina sharply, interrupting Meredith and looking askance at her vividly blazing eyes.

'Not now!' he growled.

'How *could* you?' Katarina raged. 'Our arrangement——'

'I know,' he said grimly. 'I'm sorry. It's just that I'm tired of——'

'You play with my life!' cried Katarina dramatically, wringing her hands.

'And you all play with mine,' answered Lucenzo quietly. 'Once, just this once, I would like to do what I want. I would like——'

'You can't abandon me!' Katarina said vehemently. 'I need you!'

'Tina, darling, perhaps it's time——' Lucenzo swore as Katarina interrupted him with a heart-rending wail.

Meredith put her arm around the young girl's shoulders sympathetically. 'You brute!' she said to Lucenzo, hurting for herself and for Katarina. 'You don't deserve decent women! Is Katarina your girl-friend?' she asked tightly.

'Pass.'

Her mouth thinned. 'I ought to slap your face,' she

grated. 'You dared to kiss me while she was watching? Oh! I loathe men who trifle with women's affections. Play fair, Lucenzo!'

'Remember what I told you,' he said quietly. 'Nothing is what it seems. You can't take anything I do at face value. So much is going on that you don't know anything about——'

'And don't want to,' she said coldly, 'if it involves playing a bit-part in your tortured and tangled love-life.'

'No—dammit, this is an impossible situation!' he growled.

'Nothing is impossible,' she cried furiously, disappointed that Lucenzo should turn out to be so lacking in integrity. 'Instead of playing games with us, you ought to face up to your responsibilities and the consequences of your actions——'

'I play no game! This is for real! I do nothing but think of my duty!' he snarled savagely. 'Duty rules my life——'

'Not this time, it didn't,' she glared, stroking the sobbing Katarina's hair gently. She had put aside her own longings. Katarina had fallen for Lucenzo first, that was obvious. 'You worm! You ought to be locked up, like Casanova. Look how unhappy you've made her! It's up to you to calm her down and smooth everything over.' Her whole body challenged him to defy her.

'Well, I'll be damned!'

'I wouldn't tempt the devil if I were you,' she grated.

Lucenzo gave a small smile, his eyes soft and warm and infinitely seductive. 'Do you always fight battles for those you imagine are weaker than you?'

Her stomach swooped at the grudging respect in his voice and she bit her lip unhappily, but her gaze fell on Katarina's tumbled hair and she faced up to him again. 'If you ever aspire to being a gentleman,' she said with quiet dignity, 'you must take care of Katarina.'

'And you?' he asked with low concern.

She lifted her head and glared. 'You've wounded my pride. But I've fallen on to the floor often enough to know how to get up. Look after her. She needs you more than I do.' She pushed the trembling Katarina in Lucenzo's direction.

Puzzled, he took the girl into his embrace, his piercing eyes noting Meredith's involuntary wince and her ashen face. 'It appears that you are willing to sacrifice what you want for the good of others,' he said softly.

'I don't know what you mean,' she mumbled, unable to bear the way he caressed Katarina's head.

'You talk of deception,' he said, his eyes boring into hers. 'And yet you deceive yourself.' He smiled faintly when she set her mouth stubbornly. 'Go back to my apartment. I'll find somewhere else to stay for the night,' he said softly, rocking the tearful Katarina.

Meredith swallowed miserably, imagining him comforting the beautiful girl. He would find an eager response in the devoted Katarina. 'Yes,' she said, wishing she didn't mind so much. 'I accept your offer.' She turned away disconsolately, certain she'd lost all chance of his help in finding Corosini. A long, shuddering sob broke from her lips.

'Meredith!'

Lucenzo was beside her in an instant, his hands cradling her face with the tenderness of a lover. She wrenched away from him, unable to bear the torture of it. He bewildered her with his easy lovemaking, with the sensations that he called up so easily from way inside her. They were primitive feelings which she couldn't deny. And which she never wanted to know again.

'I'm crying because I can't bear not to find my family,' she sniffed, 'not because of you.'

'I never imagined you were,' he said wryly. 'Stay in my flat for a few days and enjoy what you can of the Carnival. Here's the key.'

Her eyes were huge as she reached out and took the key from him. His hand clasped warmly around hers, detaining her as if he didn't want her to go. 'Let me go. Don't prolong this,' she said stiffly, conscious of Katarina's belligerent glare.

He looked troubled. 'Just a moment. Do you need money?'

'No!' Her head jerked up with pride. 'I'm not to be bought. I don't accept money from anyone.'

'As you wish,' he said quietly. 'But if you want cheap food, go to pizza take-aways or *tramezzini*, and eat at counters in bars. Don't buy food near San Marco. And I suggest that you use the *vaporetti*, which are very cheap——'

'Thank you,' she said stiffly, desperate to get away. 'I'm not entirely stupid. I've brought a guide book from the library. I'll manage.'

'I'll do what I can as far as the Corosini are concerned,' he said gruffly, scowling at the leap of pathetic gratitude in her eyes.

It didn't matter whether she believed him or not. He might be pretending to help her to save his face in front of Katarina and perhaps to impress her with his kindness. Whatever the reason, there was nothing she could do, other than hope. She tore her eyes away from his and pushed through the crowd, wanting only to put a great distance between herself and Lucenzo.

It was a waiting game now, she thought anxiously. And if she was staying she had to go shopping for groceries. She smiled faintly that her practical nature should surface at this moment. Life went on, whatever disappointments it brought. In the meantime she would learn all about Venice. It was her father's home, after all.

She wasn't very successful in forgetting Lucenzo, despite the excitement of the Carnival. She filled her days and nights with activities and fell exhausted into bed in the small hours, disappointed that Lucenzo hadn't contacted her. She missed him, she admitted to herself morosely. She missed being touched, and the shame of that hurt inside her like a wound.

On the Saturday, before the tourists had emerged from their breakfasts, she strolled in warm winter sunshine towards San Marco, the guide book in her hand closed for once. Her mind was taken up with puzzling over a fact which had become increasingly clear the longer she stayed in the apartment.

It wasn't Lucenzo's flat. More significant than that, no one had lived there because the sink wasn't even connected. It explained how he couldn't find switches and didn't know the layout very well. Deception seemed to be a way of life for him.

'Meredith! Come here!'

She stiffened on hearing Lucenzo's command. 'Good grief!' she cried, when she saw him. 'Prince Charming walks again!' Her astonished eyes were taking in his costume: gold-embroidered satin jacket, knee breeches and jabot of the eighteenth century. 'I feel grossly underdressed,' she said drily, indicating her close-fitting green dress.

'Sadly, you're not,' he drawled.

Irritated, she looked away and was about to tackle him about the apartment when her eyes fell on a party of very young children in fairy-tale costumes being shepherded past Quadri's *caffè* by doting parents and grandparents. Her face softened immediately, affection and wistful envy mingling in her expression.

When she turned to question Lucenzo, her breath caught in her throat at the infinite tenderness in his eyes. After a moment, he looked down on her and smiled, openly, warmly, his transparent love of children tearing raggedly at her insides.

'They've come for the children's parade,' he said softly, motioning her to a seat. 'They're all from the *ospedale*—the same orphanage I came from.'

'How old were you, then, when you were adopted?' she asked tentatively.

'Four.' He gestured towards a small boy, very solemn and proud in a gorgeous brocade coat. 'I recognise the outfit,' he said with wry humour, as the child anxiously bent to polish his black buckled shoes, the lace frothing from his sleeves.

'What a poppet he is. Oh, I do miss the kiddies in the crèche,' she sighed.

'You gave up something you really loved to look after your grandmother, didn't you?'

'Gran needed me,' she said. 'How could I do otherwise?'

'Many young women would have made a different choice,' he answered.

He was distracted by the stragglers being rounded up, and when a little girl broke away to chase a pigeon, her small hands outstretched and her face uplifted with delighted laughter, he looked ready to sweep the child up in his arms.

'You love children, don't you?' said Meredith warmly.

'Yes, I do.' His voice was guarded, but through it all she could hear the yearning and she wished she could break through the barriers he'd erected against her; she dearly wanted him to reveal his true self. 'I suppose it's bred into the Italian psyche.' His eyes strayed to the rosy-cheeked children who were chattering happily and, to Meredith's delight, he began to talk as if questioning his own feelings. 'There they are, innocent, uncomplicated and trusting, accepting the world for what it is and getting on with the business of enjoying it. When they laugh it's with sheer joy. Like you.'

She blinked. Was that a compliment? 'I know I'm naïve——'

'Pure,' he corrected. 'Uncorrupted. So far.'

'So far. . . Are you suggesting you might corrupt me?' she challenged.

'I might,' he said enigmatically.

'You should try being more like the children you

admire,' she said, sadness in her eyes. 'Instead of
being so deceitful. That isn't your flat, is it?'

'No. I didn't expect Mr Meredith Williams to stay,'
he said curtly. 'I hastily fitted it up and went through
the pretence because I didn't want him knowing where
I really live.'

'And where is that?'

'I'll take you there.'

'No, thanks,' she frowned.

'Hear my news, then.'

Excitedly, she caught his brocade sleeve. 'Lucenzo!
Have you persuaded my family that I don't have two
heads and a forked tail?' she cried, trying to joke. But
her pulses were jumping around all over the place.

'I talked to them about you,' he said slowly. 'The
main opposition is from Corosini's mother. She's
extremely hostile.'

'Why?' demanded Meredith, leaning towards him
and impatiently pushing back strands of red hair that
were wisping across her face.

Lucenzo's mouth quirked cynically. 'She was
engaged to your father, for a start.' Lucenzo fiddled
with the lace inside his deep cuffs. 'Your father jilted
her. As a matter of honour, it was agreed that she
should marry your father's brother Luigi.'

'I have an uncle?' she exclaimed.

'Had,' said Lucenzo tightly. 'He's dead.' His face
darkened. 'He died cursing your father for trapping
him into a loveless marriage,' he growled.

'That wasn't Father's fault!' she said defensively.

'He was responsible for the situation. He chose your
mother above duty.' His head lifted, presenting a pure,
stone-carved profile to Meredith. A Renaissance
prince, she thought, with an inner world no one would
ever penetrate. Her heart lurched with an indefinable
longing.

'Mother said they'd met at university——' frowned
Meredith.

'That's right. Antonio was studying business management there. Your mother was in a play near by and his head was turned by her, but she refused to leave her homeland.'

'So Father was forced to make a choice between Mother, and his fiancée and Venice,' she said, her face soft as she thought of the power of romance.

Lucenzo glared. 'He had duties to consider. As the elder son, he had responsibilities over and above those to his fiancée.'

'Go on,' she said quietly. 'I want to know it all.'

'The family were distraught when your father came back to Venice to explain that he couldn't live without your mother. This. . .actress, this woman on the make.'

'No. Mother was never grasping,' denied Meredith, 'though I can understand his parents must have thought that. How heartbroken they must have been! To lose their son. . .what a terrible thing.'

'The family bond is sacrosanct,' growled Lucenzo.

'Everyone sees things differently. Father reached out for love and didn't want to let it go. You were adopted so you must find it difficult to understand anyone wantonly rejecting what you never truly had,' she replied.

He grunted. 'You're right. You understand people very well, don't you?' he said slowly. 'You rarely condemn. Instead, you try to work out why they behave as they do. And your thinking is invariably based on love and affection.'

Meredith trembled at the tenderness in his tone. He was consciously allowing her to see his softer side, and for such a proud, private man that was perhaps the greatest compliment he would ever pay her.

'I try to put myself in other people's shoes. Imagine my father's feelings, knowing that he'd probably never set eyes on Venice again,' she said, her emotions making the words husky.

'He did come back once. I think that's when he must have deposited those items in the safety box.'

'Knowing him, I expect he wanted to get rid of anything that made him think of the separation from his family,' she said sympathetically. 'No wonder he looked wistful sometimes. What made him return that one time?'

'The death of his brother. Luigi was only thirty-one,' said Lucenzo grimly. 'He was riding on the mainland and broke his neck in a fall.'

'How sad,' she sighed. 'Did Luigi have children?' she asked tentatively. Lucenzo's chest rose and fell as if he was identifying with the loss of the Corosini family, and that touched her heart. 'Oh, yes,' she said with a half-laugh. 'Of course he did. With Luigi dead, it must have been his son who wrote to Gran, demanding the return of the key to the deposit box. He's the Corosini I'm going to meet.'

'Good deduction. Yes, you are. Like to see where your father lived?' Lucenzo asked, quite out of the blue.

Her hand tightened on his arm and the worried lines on her face vanished in an instant. 'I'd love to!' She thought of the tragic woman who'd been deserted by her father and had settled for second best. She would never do that. Her solemn gaze rested on Lucenzo's face. 'Take me there, quickly,' she urged.

'Pack,' he said curtly. 'You can stay there while you're in Venice.'

Pure joy shone in her eyes. 'Is it occupied. . .by Corosini?'

'You'll meet him.'

She felt a warm curl of happiness deep inside her. 'Thank you,' she said fervently. 'Thank you for believing in me, for giving me a chance. You've set up this meeting for me and I can't thank you enough. I'm thrilled you've done the decent thing——'

The old scowl was back on his face as if he found her gratitude uncomfortable. 'Go on,' he said irritably. 'Pack. Meet me at the lion column in the Piazetta. Know where I mean?'

'The winged lion of Venice,' she said, nodding, trying to keep calm, but longing to skip in the air. 'You see, I've been learning about the city. *A presto*,' she said happily, throwing him a dazzling smile.

He didn't respond. She ran like the wind back to the apartment and tumbled her few clothes into bags, then raced back through the back alleys to avoid the crowds and finally met Lucenzo pacing up and down by the column. He looked angry. She slowed down, remembering that Lucenzo was in control of all the strings. The realisation of her dreams was within her grasp yet he had the capacity to ruin everything.

'Come to the Paglia,' he ordered curtly. He strode away to the Bridge of Straw where sleek motor-launches jostled for position and came to a halt by one which was larger, sleeker and more opulently fitted out than the rest. Lucenzo bent to speak to the boatman.

While waiting, she gazed solemnly at the sinister Bridge of Sighs a few yards away and thought of the prisoners who'd gazed out of its thickly grilled windows, looking for the last time on the beauties of Venice before they were incarcerated—or executed for causing the displeasure of powerful nobles. She shivered, despite the pleasant warmth of the sun.

'In you get.'

Meredith regarded the motor-launch warily. Lucenzo sounded so. . .abrupt. 'Where are we going?'

'I told you. The Corosini home. We have to cross the lagoon. Hurry up. Other boats need to pick up passengers,' he rasped. 'Dammit, if you don't trust me,' he roared suddenly, 'then go home! Don't come! I can do without this hassle. I've got businesses to run——'

'You *have* got more than one job!' she exclaimed.

'I play nursemaid,' he seethed. 'Hadn't you noticed?'

Meredith stiffened, not liking his image of her. If he was nursemaid, she must be the irritating child. But she *dared* not respond. She had to smooth things over. 'I'm sorry to have made you angry. I'm sorry if I'm taking up your valuable time, but look on the bright side,' she said with unarguable logic. 'As soon as you get me and Corosini together, you can wash your hands of me, can't you?'

She stepped into the brightly varnished launch, aided by a uniformed boatman, trying not to think of the time when Lucenzo would bow out of her life. She didn't want him to go; irascible and unpredictable though he was, he had become as necessary to her as breathing.

'*Ho intenzione prenderlo*, Benito,' muttered Lucenzo sourly, taking the wheel as if he meant to handle the boat alone.

Unhappy with that, but incapable of protesting, Meredith helped the boatman to stow away her cheap carrier bags as if they were precious. '*Grazie*, Benito,' she smiled in thanks. The man opened his mouth. Lucenzo let out a warning stream of Italian, and Meredith had the distinct impression that he was telling Benito not to speak to her.

'*Tante grazie*, Benito,' Lucenzo muttered to the boatman, who handed him the keys to the ignition.

'*Prego, Principe.*'

There was an intake of angry breath from Lucenzo, and the boatman seemed filled with remorse, but he was bundled off the boat before Meredith could make sense of the man's mistake. *Principe*, she frowned, as Lucenzo started the engine and slid out into St Mark's Basin as if he was in a tearing hurry.

Prince.

She looked at the deferential and contrite figure of the uniformed boatman on the quayside, the way the other boatmen tipped their caps to Lucenzo. Yes. It meant 'prince'. Her startled blue eyes slanted to Lucenzo's haughty profile, the golden brow, the flaring, angry nostrils, the arrogance in every line of his elegant figure. She thought of the way he exuded confidence and command, how he'd earned instant respect in Florian's, the way people in the bar had respectfully treated him. . . Yet he claimed he'd been adopted. How strange.

'You're a prince!' she cried accusingly above the growl of the powerful engines.

His dark eyes flickered briefly in her direction then he set his mouth in grim lines. 'Yes,' he growled. 'I am.' He skilfully manoeuvred the motorboat past the bobbing gondolas, which were moored to a forest of striped poles. 'Damn Benito!' he said savagely.

The beautiful brocade coat stretched taut across the back, spreading to an intimidating width with his angry, indrawn breath. Meredith caught the glint of gold in the thread. Gold thread. Of course, she thought dully. What else did princes wear?

'How many more secrets do you have?' she asked heavily.

'Thousands. Luckily the boatman doesn't know them all,' he muttered.

'That's not funny!' she said jerkily. 'Talk about leading me up the garden path! Every time I turn a corner, your secrets come out and pounce on me. What's so important about concealing your title from me?'

'I dislike fuss.'

'You won't get any from me,' she said belligerently. 'A prince is only flesh and blood and skin and bone.' He shot her a dark, smouldering glance which quickened her pulses. His flesh and blood and skin and bone were all too real, all too male. 'I'm impressed by people, not titles,' she stated.

The corner of his mouth quivered. 'So I gather,' he said, reluctantly amused.

'So all that stuff about being poor and working all hours was flannel, to make me feel sorry for you——'

'Now wait a minute!' he snapped. 'That's not how it was at all. That was true. My family was impoverished during most of my youth. The wealth we have now is all due to our hard work. I swear, on my mother's head.'

'Explain,' she said, less angrily. Any man whose voice softened at the mention of his mother couldn't be all bad. 'This must be the oddest rags-to-riches tale I'm ever going to hear.'

He shifted his breech-clad legs, straddling them to keep his balance. 'Your reaction is refreshing,' he said wryly. 'You don't even look awed.'

Then she hid it well, she mused, even if her awe wasn't for his title, but for the man. Managing the boat, he was in total command, and she admired him for the ease with which he wove between the countless busy craft, the pleasure boats, gondolas and the small and large ferries, his eyes constantly alert.

'You're not a real prince,' she reminded him gently. 'You weren't born one.'

The boat lurched as his hands slackened on the wheel and it hit the wake of a speeding launch. 'No,' he agreed. 'I wasn't. I had to learn how to be one. It's been so long now that I see the title as my right.' His mouth twisted into a grimace. 'I don't like being reminded that I have not one drop of blood to link me with my family.'

'It's as well to remember one's beginnings,' she said drily. 'You'd never guess we had the same kind of humble background,' she mused. 'They must be proud of you. Is it an old family?' she asked brightly, trying to tear her mind away from the constant, destructive need to touch him.

'Twelfth century,' he said, his voice tinged with quiet pride. 'Blue-blooded enough to take an active part in ruling the Venetian empire and having the family name inscribed in the *Book of Gold*. That's a kind of exclusive medieval club. Nobles only.'

'That's quite a leap, from orphanage to high society. It can't have been easy at first.' She imagined the child Lucenzo, parading in the Piazza in his brocade coat and shiny buckle shoes one year, then finding himself part of a real-life fairy-tale the next.

'I was young. Children adapt and learn quickly. An adult would find it harder.'

'Yes,' she said slowly. 'The adjustments would be daunting.'

How could she have been so blind? she thought privately, as they began to head out to the lagoon. Lucenzo's arrogant profile was silhouetted against the medieval Venetian skyline. A little overwhelmed by the extent of his authority, she understood why she'd been drawn to him. As well as that magnetic male attraction, he exuded self-assurance; he was comfortable in his environment, and she longed to be part of it.

'I suppose your adoptive parents couldn't have children,' she said gently. 'And needed someone to carry on the family name and the title, to stop any distant relative from——'

'Yes,' said Lucenzo quickly. His eyes were fixed remotely on the horizon. 'Father wanted someone to inherit who knew Venice and had been taught the business, someone who'd been trained to the position.'

'That grand?' she said, aching from the distance opening up between them. Now she knew why he was consorting with a countess.

He sighed wearily. 'Yes. I have money and position and power. Does that attract you?' He turned his wicked eyes on her, and she was captured by their sinful promises instantly. 'You're like all the rest,' he said with disappointment, reading her helplessness with humiliating ease. 'I made the right decision,' he added grimly.

'What do you mean?' she cried in agitation. 'Lucenzo, where are you taking me? Oh, please,' she whispered, 'don't harm me!'

CHAPTER SEVEN

GRIMLY Lucenzo stared ahead, directing the boat over the glassy lagoon, leaving far behind the picture-book island of San Giorgio. Nervously Meredith gazed at the open water ahead and then back at Venice, the minarets and bell-towers, the tall palaces just a distant unfocused blur in the morning mist. Lucenzo's golden hair streaked back in the wind, emphasising the high purity of his cheekbones, and briefly his eyes lanced hers with a calculating look.

The boat sped faster and faster, between two lanes of massive wooden tripods, marking the deep-water channel through the shallows of the lagoon. People on passing boats began to shout at Lucenzo, waving him down, but he seemed not to notice.

'Slow down!' she yelled, as the boat began to buck in the disturbed water. 'What are you *doing*?'

He seemed to jerk his mind back with an effort, swearing under his breath at his lapse of concentration. Meredith passed a hand over her spray-damp face, thinking, trying to make sense of his behaviour.

'If I had any sense, I'd dump you overboard,' he growled.

Meredith felt her legs give way, and lost her balance, but Lucenzo snaked out a hand and caught her expertly, firmly pushing her against the hatch and holding her there while she regained her equilibrium.

'I'm no threat,' she whispered, quivering from Lucenzo's nearness. 'I think Gran might have demanded the money because she thought I had a right to it, but it was for love of me and despair at our poverty—her kind of rough justice.'

'Still loyal.' Lucenzo flicked dark, unreadable eyes over her appalled pale face.

'It was wrong,' she said uncomfortably, avoiding his glittering eyes. 'But my cousin knows now that, as Luigi's son, he's the only male descendant and I have no claim to anything. The blackmail is over. He can be at peace.'

'I wish that were so!' muttered Lucenzo under his breath.

'It is!' she insisted. 'He can't hold my grandmother's misguided behaviour against me when all I want is to be part of the family, to know I belong.'

She felt the light touch of Lucenzo's fingers on her forehead and flipped up her eyes. 'If your mother was half as beautiful as you, and perhaps half as persuasive, I can understand how your father was tempted to abandon everything for her pleasure,' he said throatily.

'Don't,' she whispered. 'Don't flirt with me. Remember Katarina.'

He flicked a switch and let the boat idle. It drifted close to one of the massive posts and he went to tie up, returning to the puzzled Meredith and looking down on her thoughtfully.

'Ironic, that I'm faced with a choice now,' he mused, taking her face in his hand.

Her lashes fluttered in alarm. He couldn't possibly mean a choice between her and Katarina! He scanned the empty horizon and frowned, and she quivered, suddenly afraid at the savage look in his eyes. His big body almost trembled with passion—dark, aggressive, sexual and violent, his hand seemed big enough to break her jaw.

'Don't kill me!' she breathed. 'Not when I'm so close to being happy——'

His eyes blazed with a sudden fury, and as she cringed away from him in horror he took a deep breath and ruthlessly controlled himself till nothing but the white-boned knuckles showed his internal rage. A wintry smile appeared fleetingly on his chiselled mouth.

'You fear me,' he said softly. 'But my ancestors

stopped dumping the bodies of its enemies in the lagoon years ago. I use less crude means to make people do what I want.'

She bit her lip. She was a lamb, captured by a wolf. He was a Venetian and therefore descended from men who had ruled and schemed and dominated the world for centuries.

'Like what?'

'I think you know.'

She went cold. Blue eyes met black, the unfathomable deep waters of which hid countless secrets. She was a nuisance—an unwanted problem. What did he mean to do with her? Frantically she tried to escape from his tightening grip, but he merely laughed and trapped her against the hatch with his body. They were alone in the morning mist. A cold sliver of ice slid up her spine.

Despite her fears, she tossed her head, the red hair swirling like the flames of a fire. 'You'd better tell me what you want,' she said defiantly.

'I want you,' he whispered. 'And everything that comes with you.'

Meredith shuddered with the shock. Her body flared into life with the seduction in his voice, throwing her emotions into chaos. 'You know you can't have me!' she cried in distress.

'I think I can,' he said confidently.

His mouth touched hers lightly as she opened her lips to reply. So forceful was her intended put-down that his tongue had slid inside and was teasing the softness of her mouth with its sweet erotic movements before she could adjust to what was happening to her. And by then the hunger was climbing within her, fighting all reason that was insisting she would be mad to let him take advantage of her.

She strained back, her hands scrabbling and slipping on the smoothly varnished cabin-top, humiliated at his arrogant assumption that whatever he wanted he could have just because he was a Venetian prince. He reached the hollow of her throat, passion alarmingly evident in his half-closed eyes and in the little groans of pleasure he was giving. She trembled, wanting the soft touch of his mouth and his adoration.

But he had Katarina.

Her body arched like the curve of a gondola's prow, her eyes flashing as if they were fashioned from steel. 'Is this how princes use their power and privilege?' she raged, and his hands loosened their grip on her at the fury in her face. 'You're dressed like an eighteenth-century aristocrat; don't act like one!' Her eyes glittered an ice-blue. 'You talk about choices! I choose who touches me,' she ground out. 'No man, prince or not, gets freedom of access. Katarina loves you——'

'No. And I certainly don't love her. And only a fool would think of her when you're around.' Lucenzo's hands curved into her waist, holding her firmly against him, the masculine sensuality of his mouth a terrible focus for her eyes.

'She—she spoke of an arrangement. . .what did she mean by that?'

'That's not your business,' he growled.

'Is it an arranged marriage between the two of you?' she hazarded. 'A loveless marriage? Oh, Lucenzo, you disappoint me!' cried Meredith in horror. 'If you want money——'

'Are you offering me yours?' he mocked.

'You know I have nothing——'

He gave a short laugh. 'You have a comfortable nest-egg and you have the gondola and the mask.'

'What do you mean, the gondola and the mask?' she asked, her senses alerted.

'They're worth a fortune,' said Lucenzo, watching her reactions closely. At her shocked expression, he smiled faintly. 'They're medieval.' His inscrutable eyes bored into hers. 'The Corosini were goldsmiths for centuries.'

'But the gondola was discoloured. I thought gold never tarnished?' she frowned.

'Correct. But the different colours on the gondola were achieved by the addition of ore. Copper to make a red-gold, iron for the blue, nickel to make white and cadmium and silver for the green. The mask is coated in gold leaf. It's very valuable. Take the relics and return home. You need never work again,' he said softly. 'I'll take you direct to the airport. *Now.*'

She leaned against the cabin-top, thinking that it was no wonder Lucenzo had been ready to burst a blood vessel when she'd tried the mask on! She looked towards the bag, where she'd lovingly wrapped the two priceless items, believing them to be precious— but only because they'd belonged to her beloved father.

'I want them,' she admitted. He drew away from her, his manner cold. 'They were Father's, and they're all I have of his. But. . .if they're family heirlooms then however much I want them, I must return them to the family where they belong,' she said dazedly.

Lucenzo turned his back. She thought he must be disappointed that she wasn't going home, and realised in dismay that she'd wanted him to be glad to know she was staying.

'In that case,' he said, his voice tight with strain, 'we'd better continue.'

Relief washed through her like an incoming tide. She'd said the right thing. Lucenzo cast off, heading the boat towards a lovely little island ahead, set in an expanse of flat water, shining like a silver sheet in the weak sun breaking through the mist. To her surprise, he turned the wheel towards the channel leading to the island, and as they motored slowly past one of the enormous posts she saw a name-plate on it. 'Isola Corosini'.

'My family own an island?' she gasped.

He cut the engine and let it die down before speaking again. 'When the goldsmithing business expanded in the thirteenth century, it was moved out here because of the danger of fire from the furnaces,' he explained. 'They did the same to the glass industry, which became based on the island of Murano.'

'I'm part of history,' she said, awed.

Out on a spur of rock, a fisherman was casting his line. Further on, a hundred yards off-shore, as if he were walking on the water, his companion disturbed the glass-still lagoon as he strode through the shallows over a sand bar. Meredith's eyes swept back to the island. It sat low in the lagoon, with only the crumbling brick walls surrounding the big square house and dark cypress trees to give any height, though behind the ochre building rose the bell-tower of a small church.

'The house is a sixteenth-century palace,' said Lucenzo quietly. 'Ca' Corosini.'

'And all the family live there?' she breathed happily.

'No.' Lucenzo flicked the engine into life again, breaking the spell. 'Only me.'

'*You*? You live here? But. . .you said———' Horror-struck, she stared at him with frightened eyes. 'Clever,' she said coldly. 'Now take me back. I'm not staying on an island with you!'

'It's your only chance of knowing your family,' he said complacently. 'You have to go along with this. You'll see your cousin eventually, I give you my solemn promise. His mother still needs some convincing yet. Tell me something. Suppose *you* had the right to inherit this island and the house. Would you take that inheritance from your cousin, who thinks it's his?'

'No. It wouldn't be my moral right,' she told him firmly. 'I couldn't take it from him. I'd have done exactly what I'm doing now—make contact with the family and hope they like me.'

'You would have exchanged this place for a *cousin*?' he said in frank disbelief.

She laughed. 'People are easier to talk to than bricks and mortar! I wouldn't know what to do with a palace,' she chuckled.

'You could start by furnishing it,' he said drily.

Thinking that was a dig at female priorities, she

smiled but said nothing as they chugged slowly to a small jetty. Lucenzo ran lightly to the bow and vaulted the rail, landing neatly on the jetty to fasten the rope to the black and gold-striped *bricole*, timing everything to perfection so that he could single-handedly dock the boat and kill the engine.

It was clear that he did this every day, and Meredith could imagine what a shock her letter would have been when he'd thought that Antonio's son was on his way to claim his inheritance. It must have caused an uproar! What a good thing she *wasn't* male! She would never have got this far. Lucenzo would have seen to that.

He raised up his arms to her in a flurry of lace. Still smiling from her thoughts, she placed her hands on his broad, muscular shoulders, feeling the strength of his hands lifting down her body as if it weighed nothing at all. For a moment, he held her close, refusing to let her go.

'The prince and Cinderella,' he smiled.

'Not this time. Those two married, remember?' she replied lightly, but there was an ache inside her.

'I remember.' His mouth became grim. 'Happy ever after. Take my hand. The path's uneven.'

In silence they walked hand in hand up the path. A light breeze ruffled the trees, a few birds, excited by the brief sunshine, surrounded them with the sound of trilling sopranos with the background music of softly lapping water.

'It's paradise,' she said huskily.

'It's a nightmare.' He looked down at her astonished face with darkly angled brows. Unlocking a huge wrought-iron gate, he pushed it open. 'Look,' he said simply.

She gasped. 'Heavens! It's the forest in *Sleeping Beauty*!'

'A romantic description for a jungle,' he commented. 'It gets worse.'

Meredith half ran beside him. His stride was

impatient, as if he wanted to pass through the tangled undergrowth and brambles as quickly as possible. Birds and small animals rustled unseen, disturbed by their arrival, scurrying deeper into the impenetrable thickets.

'It's in dire need of repair,' she said, when she could see the palace more clearly.

'The walls need plastering and the roof lets in the rain,' said Lucenzo, stepping over the broken hoop-tiles on the path. His hand lovingly touched the ochre-red walls.

'It must be so frustrating, seeing it decay like this,' she sighed.

Lucenzo made no comment but pushed a huge key in the great iron-studded door. She stepped inside to a chequered marble floor, swept clean and neat, with flowers on the table. She tilted her head back to see the beamed ceiling, two storeys above then followed the line of the cedar staircase, its wooden carvings almost obliterated by cobwebs. A lump came to her throat and she sat down suddenly on the safest-looking chair she could find.

'Are you all right?' frowned Lucenzo.

She swallowed and fought back the tears, dashing her hand over her eyes. 'Father lived here,' she mumbled. 'I'm in his home, learning about his past. It's a scary feeling. Do you know what sort of state the house was in then?'

'Immaculate,' he answered, stony-faced. 'If he'd stayed, it would never have got into this condition.'

'Why do you say that?'

He flicked up the tails of his brocade coat and sat beside her, stretching out his long legs. 'The business failed because Antonio left. You see, it relied on trust, the bond of a man's word and family know-how,' he explained. 'Luigi was never strong in health, and the business slid downhill fast, especially when he died.' His face twisted with bitterness.

'What's your connection with the family?' Meredith asked quietly. 'You feel for them so acutely——'

'They've been very good to me,' he said curtly.

'I am sorry, I really am,' she said sincerely, deciding she'd better not press him further. It sounded as though they'd helped him out when he was down and out.

'Come into my study,' he said briskly. 'I'll make us some coffee.'

This, at least, was habitable—clean, with panelled walls hung with old tapestries and several oil paintings. By a large antique desk was a computer terminal, fax machine and photocopier.

'Who's the woman in the painting?' asked Meredith, examining it carefully.

Lucenzo looked up from the coffee machine warily. 'Your grandmother.'

'She's fair-haired, like you!' she exclaimed.

'Your blond crusaders left plenty of evidence of their virility,' he said sardonically.

She laughed. 'I wish I could help in some way,' she mused. 'I'd willingly plunge all my earnings into the estate, but I suppose it would be a drop in the ocean.'

'What an extraordinary offer,' he said, as the tantalising aroma of freshly brewing coffee reached her nostrils.

'I'll do anything to help my family,' she said wistfully.

'Anything?'

She spun around. His face was lowered, the dark-lashed eyes hidden. But his skin was stretched taut over his cheekbones and his gritted teeth and shaking hand betrayed his tension.

'What is it, Lucenzo?' she asked compassionately. 'Tell me.'

'I wish you'd go!' he said savagely. 'Before you're hurt!'

'What do you have in store for me?' she whispered, her stomach hollow with fear.

'I could make you very unhappy,' he said in a low growl. 'I'm giving you the chance to escape. A last chance.'

His ominous words rang true. It seemed his conscience was troubling him. 'Come clean, Lucenzo,' she pleaded. 'Let me in on this mystery that surrounds Corosini. When will he come here?'

'He'll be here at the family party in a few days,' he said gruffly.

'And so will I.'

'Sit down.'

He waved her to a comfortable old armchair, and she sank into its deep cushions, curling up apprehensively on the big seat, her eyes watching him guardedly, trembling at the thought of what he had in store for her. He brought over a tray with a silver coffee service on it and a pair of exquisite bone china cups, settling himself opposite her, his face grave.

'I hate mysteries,' she said miserably.

'Patience. You must let me handle this,' he said quietly. 'This party. . . I'm snowed under with work and I've taken too much time off to be with you. Will you help me?'

She frowned, sensing that he was holding something back. 'How?' she asked, disappointed that he wasn't confiding in her. All in good time, she told herself. He'd come round.

'Help me organise the party,' he said. She was surprised, but pleased. He did need her, after all. 'I can't expect you to understand now, but it means everything to me, Meredith,' he said huskily. 'My happiness could well depend on it. People will be there from Milan, Bologna, Rome. . . Help me to organise it,' he coaxed. 'Your relatives will be delighted to know of your contribution.'

'I feel nervous now, of meeting them,' she said with a half-laugh.

'You and they will be incognito. We're all wearing masks. It will be on Fat Tuesday, *Martedi Grasso*, the last night of Carnival. You can enjoy yourself, be your natural self, and you'll never even know who you're talking to.'

'My English will give me away——'

'There'll be other English people there too. It'll be wonderful. Food, music, dancing. . .'

'You've sold it,' she said hastily, as he leaned closer, his face infinitely kissable.

He kept coming, taking a lock of her hair in his fingers, feeling its silkiness, and his voice dropped to a sexy whisper. 'We'll break down the barriers that Corosini's mother has erected,' he promised. He groaned at her radiant face. 'All they'll know is that I am escorting a companion who is totally irresistible, and they'll fall for you as I have.'

There was a breathless silence. Meredith was frozen, her mind numb as the meaning of his words sank in. 'Oh, Lucenzo, you can't——'

'I'm obsessed by you,' he muttered. He knelt beside her and clasped her hands passionately. 'You're a challenge. I've never met anyone like you before. You're totally unselfish. You care for others more than yourself.' He smiled to himself. 'You're as pure and as good as gold. You even glow like it. Nothing seems to spoil you. You're constant.'

He began to kiss her fingers, one by one, and Meredith gazed helplessly at him, knowing she loved him with such a sudden, painful realisation that she groaned aloud. 'Please don't,' she breathed, thinking of Katarina. 'What about——?'

His finger pressed her lips, his eyes warning her not to continue. 'You don't wish a loveless marriage on me, do you?' he asked gently. Meredith was torn by his predicament. 'We've known each other such a short time, but I feel I know you better than anyone. Do you feel like that too?'

Meredith gave a little helpless gasp. His finger was tantalisingly curving around her mouth. . .parting it . . .and he was kissing her gently, almost without pressure. She sat rigidly, shaking, incapable of anything other than being there, pliant in his hands.

Her fingers drifted up to touch his silky hair, and she was suddenly possessed of a fierce desire to deepen his kisses. Of their own volition, her hands tightened in his hair, forcing his head forwards, and she responded to his kiss with a passion she never knew was within her.

'Oh, Lucenzo,' she moaned, exulting at his shudder of desire and the sexy male groans he was making. More alarmed by her own terrible longing than his, she pushed against his shoulders. 'That's enough!' she said huskily.

He stood up and strode over to the window, leaving her totally confused. 'Will you help me with the party?' he asked tensely.

She swallowed so that she didn't sound as if she was shell-shocked. 'If you want,' she answered, shaken to the core.

He turned, a radiant smile on his face. 'Thank you. Perhaps we ought to have some lunch?'

'L-l-lunch?' she stammered.

'You don't know much about men, do you?' he said softly. 'I'm trying to control a wild urge to pick you up and carry you to my bedroom.'

He licked dry lips, and she found herself having to mimic his action, her eyes as dark and huge as his. She noticed the way his chest heaved, the rivers of desire flowing from him across the room to burn her body with unbearable heat. Like the furnaces, she thought crazily.

She thought of staying here the night with him, and knew she couldn't. Innocent, virginal and as strictly moral as she was, she knew that what she felt for Lucenzo was so powerful and primeval that she would never resist him. He read the truth in her limpid eyes. And took a step towards her.

'Lunch,' she croaked.

Lucenzo came to a halt. 'Yes, Meredith,' he said

meekly. But there was a secret smile beneath the bland expression, and she worried about his intentions, feeling in her heart that she could never entirely trust Lucenzo.

'Come and choose your costume,' he suggested after lunch.

It seemed an innocent enough thing to do. But when he threw open the door to a room upstairs she saw a trouser-press and a black silk robe flung on a chair and knew it was his bedroom.

'I shouldn't go in,' she said uncertainly.

He looked at her and laughed. 'Meredith! I could make love to you in any room in the house,' he grinned. 'Here, in the kitchen, on the stairs even. You're not safe anywhere, so you can hardly object to entering my bedroom.'

'Your logic is faultless.' She smiled wryly.

'It certainly is,' he agreed in amusement.

Tremulously she took his outstretched hand and it closed around hers as if it had been there forever. He took her to the foot of the elaborately draped four-poster and opened an iron-banded chest.

'These are beautiful,' she breathed, her slender fingers caressing the gorgeous fabrics as he dived into the layers of tissue and pulled out several glorious costumes. The heavy skirts rustled alluringly, and she wanted to try them all on, even the sumptuous men's coats.

'They don't make them like that nowadays,' he agreed, shaking out a scarlet Victorian ballgown.

'You mean these are all original?' She snatched her hands away, conscious of the danger of the acids on her skin which would damage old fabric.

'Of course. Look,' he said, holding up against her a dress encrusted with embroidery. 'Green is a stunning colour on you.'

'I can't,' she said, shaking her head with reluctance.

'These ought to be in a museum, Lucenzo. Without proper care they'll fall to pieces.'

'How about these? They've been made for more recent Carnivals. This one, for instance.'

Her face broke into a beautiful smile as he lifted a heavy sapphire-blue dress on to the brocade counterpane and spread the voluminous skirts. Her tutored eye saw that it had been made by a skilled seamstress, the tight, low-cut bodice erupting in a flurry of lace at the breast, the equally tight sleeves stiff with fake pearls and silver thread which formed the same flower design that was on the over-skirt.

'It would be rather revealing,' she demurred, but she knew she had to try it on. The material felt soft to her touch. It was a Cinderella dress and no mistake. She lifted the fabric to her cheek, her eyes dreamy.

'Choice of costume reveals a lot more than just cleavage. I'd love to see you in it,' he said in a low voice.

It was risky and she knew it. She eyed it, turned away, and then glanced back longingly. 'Perhaps there's something. . .more. . .formal?' she said, dragging the words out with ill-hidden reluctance.

Lucenzo's dark eyes mocked her cowardice. He went over to the bed, lifted up the skirts and the separate bodice and draped them over his arm, pushing Meredith in front of the ornate Venetian gilt mirror complete with cherubs and vine leaves that occupied a good twenty feet of wall space.

He held the dress against her, his heavy arm pressing into her body to nip in the waist realistically. Slowly his eyes toured the skirts and the bodice, which her hands had draped in place. Behind her, she felt him quiver, his breath lifting her hair.

'If any dress was made for you, this was it,' he said softly.

It shouldn't have made that much difference to the way she looked, but it did. Something in the quality and the texture of the fabric—the colour, too, brought

out the porcelain of her complexion. The pearls—fake
though they must be—added a glow which echoed the
delight in her face.

'I've got to try it on, even if I decide on something
less saucy,' she laughed, her eyes alight with
excitement.

His grin flashed in the mirror. 'I can never understand people who've been brought up in your country.
Why be ashamed of beauty? Your body is perfect. Let
the world know that.'

She blinked in surprise and blushed with his flattery.
'Showing off seems to be the thing to do in Venice,'
she retorted wryly. She had no intention of telling him
that she wouldn't feel safe with him if she wore
anything vaguely provocative. 'I don't know. . .'

His eyebrow crooked in amusement. 'I'm dressed as
a prince. Be my princess for the afternoon. I'll show
you the rest of the house and you can live a dream for
a while.'

'You're appealing to my love of fairy-tales,' she
chided. 'But yes. I'd love that.'

'Let me know when you're ready,' he said huskily.
'I'll be outside. Those are the petticoats. You put that
short one *over* the long ones to make the skirts stand
out.'

'Yes, I know. I've worked with costumes, remember?' She took the dress and laid it on the bed again.
She badly wanted to ask how he knew so much about
dressing women, but controlled her curiosity. It
sounded like petulant jealousy, she thought with a
sigh. He must have kissed so many women . . . She bit
her lip.

His grin slashed his face. 'Don't change your mind—
I couldn't bear it! Hurry up. I'm an impatient man. I
don't usually wait outside while women take their
clothes off.'

'Casanova,' she flung at him darkly.

'I'm flattered. He was a superlative lover,' Lucenzo

murmured. He gave her a knowing, triumphant look and softly closed the door behind him.

Left alone, Meredith ignored her shaking legs and managed to strip off and ease herself into the heavy waist petticoats from beside the chest. But, to her surprise, when she tied them at the back they were hardly any weight at all. The dress was more difficult. She managed to slip the skirt over her head gingerly and settle it in place with its ribbon ties, but she realised that she needed a maid to lace up the front of the separate bodice for her.

'I'm ready,' she called, making do with holding it firmly around her like a waistcoat and sucking her breath in hard. 'What do you think?' She tipped her head on one side, judging the effect. The lacy bra straps spoilt the effect.

'Terrible. Come here.' With an aggressive movement, Lucenzo turned her around to face him and pulled the lower lace tight.

'No, it's all right——' she cried, flushing when she felt the warmth of his fingers on her bare skin.

'It isn't,' he growled, his eyes hooded. 'Wear it properly.'

He pushed the bra straps off her shoulders and she looked at him helplessly, torn between releasing the bodice to grab his hands and keeping it safely in place.

'I can—get the—general idea,' she said jerkily.

He stared challengingly into her eyes, his fingers ruthlessly unsnapping her bra strap at the back. 'One of us is going to take this off,' he said hoarsely. 'I've decided it'll be me.'

Meredith felt a quiver of fear and buried it fast. 'Think again,' she said jauntily, her eyes dark with warning. 'Turn your back.'

'You've got ten seconds.'

'We've done that scene before,' she smiled.

'Eight.'

'Oh!' Hurriedly she wriggled out of her bra and drew the bodice around her full breasts just in time.

Lucenzo finished his unnervingly fast count-down and came to stand in front of her, commandeering the laces again despite her protests.

He was silent, concentrating on pulling the tight bodice in, his thick lashes a pair of dark fluttering crescents on his high cheekbones. Meredith's soft blue eyes lingered on them, feeling a tug of pleasure in the contrast of vulnerability and strength in his face. She trembled with a vivid awareness that was tingling through her whole body, bringing warmth to her skin and champagne into her bloodstream.

Tense muscles played around his jaw; he scowled at the stubborn laces and tugged. She lost her balance and fell against him, feeling the muscular body tense and brace itself to stop her falling further. His lashes quivered but didn't lift, and she saw that his lips had parted to reveal his teeth.

'Put your hands on my shoulders,' he grated.

'Yes, Lucenzo.' She stared, hypnotised, not daring to move again as he resumed his task, and she fought her physical responses, rigidly blocking out the sensual touch of each curling finger as it hooked up the criss-crossing lace. But nothing could stop her from breathlessly anticipating the next light, accidental caress.

'Dear God!' he muttered, his fingers fumbling.

'I can do the last bit,' she said hastily, exerting a steely self-control. His expression was unreadable, but she knew from the hot breath flowing over her breasts that he was finding the procedure as erotic as she was.

'Have a look,' he grated in an unnervingly hoarse voice.

She knew why he sounded so strangled when she saw herself. Flushed, lit from within, with her copper hair softly spread over her bare shoulders, she was exposing more flesh than she had realised. The tight lacing had thrust her breasts up and out, creating a deep cleavage and the impression of a voluptuous, sensual woman beneath the formal yet sexy costume. Her waist looked even smaller with the great spread of

the skirts and the blueness of her eyes was more
intense than she'd ever known.

Puzzled, she stared at herself. There was more. An
awareness of herself. A kind of mysterious allure—
expectation, confidence.

Her eyes flickered for a split-second to see Lucenzo's
reaction. There was a white line around his mouth and
he was watching her with undisguised lust, as if he
wanted her and hated himself for being so human.

'I don't think——' she whispered.

'Oh, I do.' He came close behind her, their eyes
locking like laser-beams on one another in the mirror.
His face was guarded now, much to Meredith's relief.
'I think you will be a sensation.'

'I'm supposed to melt into the background——'

'You said you'd help me. Wear that dress and be my
partner. Leave the rest to me.'

'It sounds fishy,' she said unhappily. 'I won't be part
of any deception.'

'No. You won't. I promise you.' His hands rested
lightly on her shoulders and she shivered. 'You'll have
to do better than that,' he said huskily.

'What—what do you mean?'

'At the party, you must behave as if you like me.'
His voice sounded thick with hunger, deep and growl-
ing as if he wanted more from her. 'The Corosini will
be sure to talk to you then, because they'll be
interested in the woman I've brought. That is,' he said
hoarsely, 'if we ever get out of this bedroom again.'

With an awful sense of panic, Meredith realised her
position. Through her own trusting innocence she was
alone with a man who'd stated quite clearly that he
wanted her. On an island, inches from his bed, dressed
as provocatively as possible. She opened her mouth to
speak.

His head slowly tilted and she watched, mesmerised,
as it angled sideways, then she felt his warm lips on
her neck like a brand. I'm his. I love him, I want him,
she thought wildly. But I daren't surrender. . .daren't

weaken. . . He was using her to advance himself somehow, for the sake of his family, and he intended to bind her to him before the party, so that he could demand her total loyalty.

She tried to speak again but her vocal cords produced only faint strangled sounds. 'Lucenzo,' she mouthed, her eyes watching the slow downward crawl of his hands.

Robbed of speech and of movement, it was all she could do. Down went his fingers, down her arms to her elbows, cupping them in his palms, feeling the smoothness, while all the time his mouth explored the nape of her neck, the small bones down her spine to the sensitive areas of her upper back.

She strained away, but saw that her breasts were thrust out further, and now she had a new sensation to worry about—the liquid feeling in her loins as if he'd built a small fire there. His fingers were spanning her tiny waist, smoothing inexorably up the fabric of her bodice, shaping over the curves where her breasts swelled out like ripe melons ready for him to taste.

But his lips were busy elsewhere, his teeth gently savaging her shoulder, and then a more violent devouring of the soft flesh at her neck again brought a gasp of need to her parched throat. Still no sound escaped, only a rush of panic-stricken breath.

She made a little moan, her head refusing to obey her and tilting back in pleasure at the touch of his hands. He lifted his head and stared at her, the incredible primitive light in his eyes fanning the small fire within her into an inferno. She pleaded silently. Relentlessly, his dark eyes flaring with sexual menace, he pulled her against him, his hand pressing on the naked cushions of her soft white breasts. And then his fingers had slid into the bodice, ruthlessly jerking the laces free, his face harsh with determination.

'Oh, no,' she whispered, her voice released with her breasts. To her horror, she saw that they were exposed to his avid gaze. Swollen, tight and capped with two dark, elongated peaks, her breasts didn't seem to belong to her. They were too eager for his hands, too ready to leap into a fierce throbbing as he groaned harshly in his throat with pleasure and delicately manipulated the rosy tips with his finger and thumb.

He was a sensualist, she thought in despair. She should have realised that earlier. With treacherous defiance, her eyes closed, abandoning her to her fate like the rest of her body, and she felt a despair that her brain was so languid that it wasn't helping her to deny him.

'God,' he breathed. 'You excite me beyond all control.'

'It's not me, you're reacting to the dress,' she husked painfully. 'Ohhh!' She shuddered at the pressure of his fingers. Wilfully, her ribcage lifted, offering itself.

'It's you,' he growled, roughly turning her around and catching her shoulders in his hard grip. 'It's what you are beneath the face you show to the world. The woman, full of passion, need, loving.'

His mouth prevented her from replying, violently possessing her lips while his hands roughly sought to drag off her bodice completely.

'Lucenzo, Lucenzo,' she moaned, twisting her head away.

'No, you can't stop me. I want you and I will have you,' he said passionately.

The colour left her skin, her pale face showing a deep fear at the way he was crushing her to his body, the whipcord strength of his arms and the determination of his roaming fingers giving her an idea of the violence with which he would take her.

His leg thrust into the volume of her skirts so that it was hard against her pelvis, and even through the multitude of petticoats she could feel the hard, rigid evidence of his ungovernable arousal as he straddled her thigh.

The passion of his kisses on her throat were leaving her weak and she had to will her fingers to hold on to the bodice. Fiercely his mouth soared over her face, her eyes, her cheekbones, her jawline. . . She began to find breathing almost impossible, and tossed her head this way and that to escape his remorseless onslaught.

For a moment she found her lips on his smooth cheek, and she tasted salt from the spray of the boat journey. Her mouth lingered, a little too long. For she had taken her mind from his marauding hands and, with a low guttural cry, he had succeeded in stripping off her top and flinging it from them into the dark recesses of the room.

Backing away, her eyes dark with fear and a terrible, raging need as he prowled, step by step, towards her, she felt her naked spine against the chill glass of the mirror.

He smiled slowly and held her prisoner with his eyes while he removed his jacket with an almost leisurely air. His fingers flipped open the buttons of his waistcoat.

Meredith almost crumpled from the erotic sensuality of his practised movements. 'You can't force me,' she whispered, protecting her nakedness with her hands, each breast splayed in a plump cushion around her spread fingers. He touched his lips with his tongue and, to her horror, her palms felt the nub of each breast thrust in hungry demand.

'But I can persuade you,' he said, his eyes slumberous. 'Long and slow and tantalisingly painful.'

'Pain. . .' She gulped. 'Painful?' she croaked. He'd said he would hurt her. . .

'The waiting,' he said softly. 'The beautiful torment of denial, of postponing the inevitable and building up a sweet need that improves every second of surrender. I've been waiting for this for so long that I don't think I can wait any longer——'

'Lucenzo. . .' Her eyes were crystalline with panic. 'Did—did you bring me here on purpose?'

'Yes,' he growled savagely. 'Of course.'

She winced at his ruthless manipulation, and he moved forwards quickly, confounding her by kneeling and pulling away her hands, holding them by her sides, the weight of his body pressing against her as his mouth came inexorably closer towards her pulsating nipple.

She wanted to feel his lips there, wantonly betrayed by her own unleashed desires, the pulses of arousal singing in her body, every nerve jerking with the intolerably slow progress of his mouth.

'Oh, Cenzo,' she whispered helplessly. 'Cenzo, Cenzo, Cenzo!'

The thick fringe of lashes flicked up, and she felt herself melt into him, slowly reaching out with her hand to caress his impassioned face. Her hand drifted to the back of his head and without any conscious decision of her own it pressed lightly to bring his mouth to her aching, demanding breast.

She felt the shudder within him, felt a pride and an elation that she had caused it, then could think of nothing other than the exquisite sensations shooting through her body, radiating to every part of it and suffusing her with an unstoppable arousal. His moist mouth suckled, and when she gazed down at his rapt, contented face she knew that she was lost to him.

Warm, tense with desire, she tried to reason with herself, to find the words to stop him. And couldn't think of a reason why she should. Shocked at her lack of morals and the ease with which he'd reduced all her defences to nothing, Meredith moaned and tried to push him away.

'Impatient?' he growled.

At the same time as he stood up he slid his hands beneath her skirts and let them rise up her legs to her thighs, his face quite wickedly triumphant at his own cunning.

'No, Lucenzo!' she said in despair, alarmed that he'd misunderstood her.

He ignored her, lifting her with his strong arms on

to the bed, his hands still on her thighs and dangerously moving inwards where her own fires burned
unchecked, waiting to be extinguished.

'Undress me,' he whispered. 'Look at us—we could
be two eighteenth-century lovers.'

'But we're not lovers,' she mumbled. 'There's no
love——'

'This will do very well for the moment,' he murmured, nibbling her ear, his hands finding at last the
soft flesh between her thighs. He let out a deep,
hungry growl as she bucked and gasped from the
shocking sensation, her eyes like a frightened doe's.

'But not for me!' she cried unevenly, startled and
dismayed by her body's need. The throb his touch was
arousing was like concussion blows vibrating through
her veins. 'Please, Lucenzo, please don't,' she moaned
in desperation. 'Not any more—I can't bear it——'

'I can't either,' he muttered harshly. 'You can't ask
me to stop. It would be too cruel when we——'

Meredith pressed her thighs together as tightly as
she could, summoning up all her resolve. 'Crueller to
make me do what you want,' she said in an unnaturally
high voice.

'Coax. Seduce. To do what you want too. I want
you to be eager,' he muttered in savage passion. 'To
be as demanding as me, to lose yourself in my arms
and to hell with the rest of the world. Let's take what
pleasure we can, when we can.'

She clung to the last vestiges of reality. 'I can't,' she
whispered.

Effortlessly, his knee slid to part her legs, but when
she threw him a look of utter dismay he paused.
'*Carissima*. Why not?' he asked quietly, his breathing
suspended.

'I told you. I must be a virgin when I get married!'
she said shakily, begging him with a terrified
desperation.

For a moment he didn't move an eyelash. Then his
face contorted in pain, and she knew instinctively with

infinite relief that it was the face of a man reluctantly
denying himself the sexual release he patently craved
by wielding a superhuman control.

'Oh, Meredith!' he groaned. Abruptly he left her,
the bed lifting as he rose, and began to stride up and
down the floor while Meredith frantically searched for
her own clothes, her eyes warily on him. 'I've got to
take you back to the mainland,' he grated, turning to
face her. She blushed, caught with her engorged
breasts exposed while she tried to hook up her bra
with nerveless fingers. 'Here. I'll do that——'

'No!' she yelled.

'It's over,' he said wearily. 'For you, anyway. I'm
perfectly capable of controlling myself if it's absolutely
necessary.' He gave a bitter smile. 'I've had *years* of
practice.' Ignoring her protests, he snapped the hook
into place and adjusted the straps for her comfortably,
as if he'd dressed thousands of women.

A fierce, murderous jealousy lanced through
Meredith. She kept her eyes downcast so that he
wouldn't see its telltale signs, and sullenly dressed
while he continued to pace up and down, probably
trying to release some energy. She was innocent of the
intimate ways of men and had no idea how long it took
them to relinquish their needs.

But she knew it would take a while before the
immeasurable hunger receded within *her*. She burned
and throbbed as if she had a fever.

'Take me back to Venice now,' she husked, wrig-
gling her thighs to dissipate the ache.

Lucenzo's avid eyes saw the movement and glittered, but he nodded and went downstairs. She followed slowly, feeling hot and tense. Seeing his broad
back and shoulders, the proud carriage of his dark
head, she felt an overwhelming longing to give in to
her clamouring body.

If he'd looked around and fixed her with his melting
eyes, she might have done. But he walked on ahead
and out of the front door. Where he stopped.

The moment she came to the top step, she realised
what the matter was. Fog was creeping in over the
island and in the distance the deep boom of a foghorn
sounded, echoing her own sudden melancholy.

'We'd better hurry!' she said anxiously, running
down the steps.

He didn't move. 'We can't go in this.'

'What?' She confronted him, her hands on her hips.
'We *have* to. I can't stay here with you.'

'I don't think I can stay here with you either,' he
muttered savagely, 'but I have no choice. Look at it,'
he grated. 'Damn fog; it's rolling in as if it means to
isolate us beneath a blanket.'

She flinched at his ill-judged choice of words. 'It
might be all right by the jetty,' she argued, running
down the path. Before she'd gone very far, she could
see that this wasn't like the fogs she knew. It was
dense, almost a white-out. Damp and shivering, she
stared with growing dismay as it hid the end of the
jetty and seemed to be threatening to obscure her own
feet. 'Lucenzo!' she yelled.

'*Tranquilo*. I'm here. You do see how it is, don't
you?' he said curtly.

'This is terrible! Do you have some kind of contact
with the weather gods?' she asked sourly.

'You're supposed to be Miss Sunshine,' he snapped.
'You clear it away.'

He turned on his heel, and she stumbled after him,
not wanting to be alone in the eerie garden where even
the birds had been subdued by the fog.

'You're angry?' she asked.

'No. Yes. Oh, not with you,' he sighed. 'With
myself, and the fog and the whole damn Corosini
family. Duty! Just for once I'd like to do what I
choose.' He slammed the door behind them furiously,
his face thunderous in its anger. 'As for now. . .what
the hell are we going to do with ourselves?'

CHAPTER EIGHT

EVENTUALLY, after some awkward silences in the kitchen while they grimly drank endless cups of coffee, they settled for organising the party. Meredith lost herself in the arrangements, and between them they managed to create a reasonable atmosphere again. Yet every time he laughed and his grin dazzled her she flinched with the deep-rooted need that stabbed like a vengeful sword.

Later, he showed her around and told her in detail the things that needed doing to the house, and she imagined her father here, sliding down the banisters or across the ballroom floor, and she felt a sentimental attachment to the place creep over her like the muffling fog.

Lucenzo built a log fire in the big medieval fireplace, and they sat burning their toes on the stone hearth. Outside, unhindered by curtains, and with the shutters broken, she could see the fog rolling into the windows.

'It looks as if the fog wants to come in,' she said absently.

'I don't blame it,' said Lucenzo softly. 'It can see contentment in here.' He turned to look at her, and the sweet, warm smile that lit his face made her heart contract. He saw it—somehow—she didn't know how, because his voice trailed away into nothing. 'Meredith, I'm crazy about you,' he said in his golden honey voice, a wayward lock of hair falling over his forehead.

The words glided over her, flowing into her very being, seeping into her own heart with a cruel accuracy. She had already fallen in love with him, her whole heart had been surrendered, but he could never know that because he would have such power over her that she would never be able to deny him her body. And they still had the night to get through.

'Don't——'

'I need you,' he said softly, his eyes devouring her tense face.

Her defences collapsed. She sat there, quivering as he took her in his arms, kissing her so sweetly that she thought the pain of love would tear open her heart. There was such comfort, such happiness with him that she could only sigh with pleasure. 'Cenzo,' she mumbled.

'Do you love me?' he murmured, his mouth exploring her ear.

She nodded dumbly. He held her at arm's length and smiled tenderly. 'Say it,' he coaxed. 'I want to hear you say it. *Ti amo*.'

'I love you, Lucenzo,' she whispered. 'I love you. *Ti amo*.'

Gently he released her and stood up. 'There'll be a surprise for you at the party. *Dormi bene*. Sleep well.'

She sat immobile for a long time, staring into the embers of the dying fire, her thoughts so chaotic that she could hardly make any order out of them. Instinct told her that he was planning something for her and it might not be to her liking. She shivered at the chill which stole over her body.

The fog continued to enclose them in their own world for the whole of the next day, deadening all sound outside so that it seemed as if everything was hushed and waiting. With regular monotony the fog-horn sounded, its mournful sound doing nothing to squash Meredith's high spirits.

'Did you get on to the contract cleaners?' she asked Lucenzo, working through her check-list. She planned, he phoned. They worked well together, she thought wistfully.

'Yes. And the interior decorator will come tomorrow—fog allowing—to hang drapes,' he said.

'Good.' Meredith leaned forwards to the chart she'd

made and ticked those items off. 'The caterers are coming in during the afternoon. Gardeners?'

'Can't we have lunch?' he murmured hopefully. Meredith simply continued to eye him steadily, and he chuckled. 'And I thought you were sweet and gentle,' he said ruefully. His face was dissolving into laughter, and she dearly wanted to throw her arms around him. 'I'm dying of hunger here,' he complained.

'We finish our schedule first,' she said firmly. 'That's how you get things done. Distractions aren't allowed.'

'Then you'd better throw a blanket over your head,' he said quietly. 'Because I want to kiss that prim look off your face.'

She blinked and tried to hide her longing for him. 'Please, Lucenzo,' she implored. 'One of us has to be sensible——'

'For the first time in my life, it doesn't have to be me,' he said huskily.

'You've worked very hard to get where you are, haven't you?' she observed sympathetically.

He stretched to ease his limbs from a morning spent at the desk. 'All the other kids went out to play. I stayed in and studied,' he reminisced. 'I knew that I had to be the best at everything if I was to haul my family out of the financial trouble they were in. I vowed that my brothers would never go hungry.'

'You never said anything about brothers!' she cried in delight.

He smiled gently. 'My blood brothers. We were adopted as a package. They'll be at the party.'

'Tell me about them. I want to meet your family as much as mine,' she said.

He laughed. 'Just as well! Rizzi works on the land, Fonzi with horses.'

Meredith was entranced by the softness of his face. 'You love them very much.'

'I would die for them.' She felt his warm mouth on the palm of her hand then she was being pulled on to his lap. 'Your heart,' he marvelled softly. His fingers

lightly touched her breast and he smiled. 'It's hammering as violently as mine,' he whispered shakily. 'You
do love me, don't you, *amore*?'

'Yes. I do,' she whispered. His mouth began to
nuzzle her face, and she waited for him to declare
himself. In vain. 'Lucenzo, there's so much to be
done!' she complained helplessly.

With a show of regret, he slid her on to her own
chair again. 'Gardeners,' he said sternly to himself,
clearing his husky throat. 'I'll get them to cut a swath
through the brambles to widen the path and save the
costumes from snagging. Your face is so beautiful, I'm
thinking of finding a mask for it so that I can get
through the day. . . And I've asked them to bring a
boatload of garlands——'

'Lucenzo!' she remonstrated. 'Garlands will cost the
earth!'

'Yes. And your eyes——'

'Don't!' she moaned. 'You are impossible! Tell me
. . .this party is important to you, isn't it?' she asked
anxiously.

His face was grave. 'For you and me both.' And he
wouldn't explain that remark, no matter how much
she pestered him.

The fog lifted and the house became filled with a
babble of excitable people, few of whom spoke English
and who all arrived at once because they'd been
waiting for a clear passage. Meredith found herself an
interpreter—the son of the cook—and he'd become
her devoted fan.

'You're doing brilliantly,' smiled Lucenzo, waylay-
ing her in the dining-room, his arms full of hyacinths.

She inhaled the heady perfume to avoid looking into
his compelling eyes. 'I'm on wings,' she admitted. 'It's
wonderful, seeing the palace brightened up. I wish I
had the money to help my cousin restore it.'

'Nice thought. What the——?' Lucenzo moved
away and began to complain to the catering manager,

breaking into the man's spirited singing of an Italian opera.

'*Basta*! *Basta*!' cried the manager excitedly, trying to stop Lucenzo from moving the tables.

'He say enough, enough,' said Mario the kitchen boy helpfully.

'I got the drift,' murmured Meredith. 'Lucenzo, what are you doing?'

'I want the tables over there,' he said calmly. 'Come over here.' Lucenzo swept over to her, caught her arm and dragged her to the entrance of the ballroom. 'Look. The view.'

'Stunning,' she said, admiring the rich purple drapes and acres of gold bunting and surreptitiously easing away from his warm body. Someone was balancing precariously on a ladder, inserting four-foot candles into gilt sockets on the wall while his partner was hanging gold balloons and purple streamers below. It looked like a fire hazard. 'We need buckets of water,' she said to young Mario.

'Pay attention to me!' frowned Lucenzo. 'I don't want the guests to see this till they've eaten. Feed them first, stun them later. You never reveal your complete hand at the beginning. Show a little at a time,' he smiled.

'That sounds like you,' she said ruefully. 'But if the doors are shut no one will hear the orchestra in the ballroom,' she argued.

'They will. Because we're having two orchestras. Quartets. Period music. Our guests eat, chatter, listen to Vivaldi. At the right moment we fling the ballroom doors open, there's the sound of a spinet, the room is ablaze with candlelight——'

'It sounds fabulous. We move the tables,' she laughed, capitulating.

To quell a riot, she kept a sympathetic hand on the manager's arm while the young boy repeated her instructions. When the man bristled, she looked at him imploringly and he threw up his hands in a tirade of explosive Italian. But she coaxed him along with her unwaveringly sympathetic smile, and he ordered everyone to dismantle the tables and re-set them.

'You gave him a look he couldn't refuse,' mused Lucenzo. 'No wonder everyone is singing while they work. I expected this place to be in chaos—instead, it's an oasis of calm. You could easily run a house like this.'

She flushed with his praise, happy that his party looked like being a success. 'I learnt organisation from Father,' she said softly. 'I helped him to give parties. Even when I was little I ran around helping. Like Mario here,' she said, hugging the boy's thin, strong shoulders.

Mario almost burst with pride. 'I am. . .' His eyes searched Meredith's anxiously, as he tried to get his tongue around the word she'd taught him.

'In. . .val. . .' she prompted.

He grinned. 'Invallyball,' he said, stalking off to supervise a pretty maid while Meredith and Lucenzo tried not to crush his self-confidence by giggling aloud.

'You're good with people from all walks of life,' commented Lucenzo thoughtfully. 'People love working for you. Your orders are clear and sensible and without arrogance, and you have a great enthusiasm for everything you do.'

'You're a flatterer,' she teased, a little rueful that he didn't entirely mean what he said. It was expansive talk, nothing more. 'Now out of my way,' she scolded. 'Go and hack down some brambles.'

'Will I be able to kiss the Sleeping Beauty if I do? I think that's what princes do for a living,' he said hopefully.

'Why not?' she laughed. 'When I've learnt your dark secrets.'

He stared at her bleakly for a moment then turned on his heel. Meredith sat down with a thump. Secrets, she thought, feeling a cold, clammy fear crawling down her neck. He was involving her in something that was tugging at his conscience.

For the rest of the afternoon and early evening Lucenzo avoided her, and her nerves reached breaking-point. She felt only an empty hollow feeling of unhappiness that nothing, not even the combined efforts of the increasingly affectionate team of workers, could dispel.

On Fat Tuesday, Meredith watched the banners being unfurled in the ballroom with a stab of pride in her heart. When she turned to go upstairs and change, she saw Lucenzo leaning against a pillar, watching her from a few yards away. And whatever he was planning for her, she didn't care. She loved him so deeply.

'I'm happier than I've been for years,' she said quietly. 'This was my father's family home, and I'm a Corosini. If I ever lived a fairy-tale, this must be it.'

'Go and get on your finery. Tonight you'll be my princess,' he said huskily.

They faced each other, and she found it hard to believe that he could be involved in anything underhand. And yet. . .'What else will happen?' she mumbled.

'You'll discover my true feelings for you,' he said in a low tone.

'Sounds ominous.'

'I want you,' he replied, his body very still. Only his eyes burned in the flawless face. 'I want *everything*. Be patient, *amore*.' He gave her a slow smile. 'It's the night for being unmasked. I shan't hide behind a disguise any more.'

'I hope you're not going to turn from a prince into a frog,' she said with a shaky laugh.

'You could kiss me now and find out.'

'No. I'll go and change,' she said, her stomach churning.

While she did so, she could hear the launches tying up and the sound of laughter. Half in excitement, half in a state of nervous panic at the thought of the momentous occasion, she pushed open the shutters to peer into the starlit night.

The path glowed in the mysterious glimmer of tiny fairy lights which disguised the presence of the jungle beyond. Piano music rippled out into the night as the richly costumed guests began to chatter and exclaim at the torch-lit façade and its huge swags of greenery laced with balloons and ribbons.

She could hardly dress, her fingers were trembling so much. Perhaps she didn't want to learn the truth. Perhaps she didn't want to meet her family. Perhaps. . .

'Meredith! Are you dressed?'

'Y-y-yes. . .'

'You're needed!' called Lucenzo sharply.

Sickness gnawed at her insides. 'In a minute!'

'Now.' The door swung open to reveal an imperious-looking Lucenzo, resplendent in coat and breeches of gold *tissu*, his white frilled cravat a perfect foil for his bronzed features. He rapped his gold-knobbed cane on the floor. 'Now,' he repeated.

'I'm scared,' she said in a small voice.

'You cope with organising a party for a few hundred people, and you're scared?' he said in disbelief. 'Put your mask on. You'll feel OK then. You look wonderful,' he said more gently. 'There'll be no one anywhere near as lovely.'

'Thank you,' she smiled shyly, and his eyes kindled.

'Your smile lights the whole room,' he murmured. 'If the candles fail, I'll have you stand in the middle radiating a little glow and we'll all dance around you.'

'Idiot!' she laughed, her heart thudding at his compliments.

'That's better. Just be yourself. They can't fail to adore you.' He held out his mask. 'Fix this for me?' She came over, but he caught her outstretched hand and bowed low over it, touching it with his lips. 'Thank you,' he said simply, then he kissed her mouth lightly.

'*Prego*,' she answered graciously. She steeled herself to touch him, taking the mask from his hand and placing it firmly on his face, looping the ribbon carefully over his ears and sweeping around him in her long skirts to tie it firmly. He removed his tricorn hat from under his arm and wedged it on his be-ribboned wig. 'I'll come in a moment.' She hesitated, then placed her hand on his arm to detain him and reached up on tiptoe to kiss his papier-mâché cheek.

'This mask could ruin my style,' he complained.

She grinned and pushed him out, glad that it had been Mario's little maid and not Lucenzo who had helped her to dress earlier. Her need for Lucenzo hadn't gone. When he'd appeared just now, her whole body had burst into life. Yet she dreaded the next few hours.

She paced the floor, waiting until she judged the rooms would be full of people. The little orchestra was playing a minuet when she began to descend the sumptuously draped stairs. She nearly ran up again when the milling throngs of people in the hallway below turned as if drilled by some invisible sergeant and stared at her.

Lucenzo detached himself from the crowd and ran up the stairs two at a time, seeing that she'd frozen. 'Make it to the bottom and you get a purple heart,' he grinned.

'I'll settle for one that beats normally,' she said breathily. 'Oh, heavens,' she groaned, seeing the visions below. 'Look at the stunning ballgowns!'

'What's a Versace or two compared with a Corosini costume?' he said encouragingly. 'Remember, behind that mask of yours, no one can tell if you're nervous.' He pressed her fingers. 'For me,' he urged. 'Do it for me because you love me.'

Slowly her head turned to him and her eyes smiled at his. 'Of course,' she said huskily.

She lifted her multi-petticoated skirts and walked down with as much grace as she could manage, playing the part of Cinderella at her first ball, prevented from any sudden movement by the flattering silken wig whose curls were interlaced with pearls and fell in tumbling ringlets on to one breast.

Men seemed to float up to her, encircling her before she reached the bottom step, and she felt Lucenzo's fingers leave hers as he was crowded out. She looked down on the men's masks and costumes, listening to their chatter, and stayed silent.

They cleared a space for her on a twelve-foot lyre-backed couch and vied to sit with her, while others took it upon themselves to disappear for food and champagne.

'*Permesso*?'

She inclined her head graciously, permitting the paparazzi to photograph her. Other masked revellers bowed to her elaborately, and still she kept silent, even when a servant, dressed like an Alice in Wonderland flunkey, presented her with a straw for her flute of champagne.

'*Principessa.*' A dashing man swept off his three-cornered feathered hat and bowed deeply to her.

She nodded and pushed the straw under her mask, sipping the champagne. The man audaciously took her hand, examined it and laughed.

'British?'

'Oh! Yes!' she chuckled, peering at her hand. 'Is it written down there?'

'I am an expert on women's hands. I first thought, Irish. The skin is so white. You are red-haired, yes, princess?'

'I am,' she said ruefully. 'Thank you,' she said warmly to the young men who had brought her plates of food. 'I'm not sure how I'm going to eat this,' she complained. 'Do you think I can get a fork under my mask?'

'Move over, Rizzi;' growled a familiar voice. 'If anyone's feeding Cinderella, I am.'

'Cenzo, you old rogue! You take the duties of an elder brother too far——'

'Katarina's in the *galleria*,' muttered Lucenzo.

'My Katarina? *Mille grazie!*' Lucenzo's brother touched Lucenzo's arm in thanks and vanished through the crowd.

'It was Rizzi!' she whispered, pleased that she'd met him. 'He's nice. Are he and Katarina lovers?'

'Hush. It's a secret for the moment.'

A great weight lifted from her mind. She'd got her lines crossed. Katarina was Rizzi's girl, not destined for a society marriage after all. 'You were terribly unkind to her,' she remembered, puzzled.

'I had to be,' said Lucenzo gently. 'She's young and very rich, and her parents disapprove of Rizzi because he doesn't have noble blood. I offered to escort her so that she could make assignations with Rizzi. Her parents didn't dare to challenge me.'

'Oh.' Her face fell beneath the mask. 'They'll have to come out into the open some time,' she said anxiously, worrying for the two young lovers.

'Gentle Meredith,' he said huskily. 'That's exactly why I read Katarina the riot act when you left. Either she had the courage of her convictions and stood up to her parents, or she wasn't good enough for my brother.'

'That's a bit tough,' she protested.

He gave an elegant shrug. 'The women in my family must be. You have to take what you want in this world,' he husked, his eyes reducing her to weakness. Without taking his eyes from her, he reached out and removed a plate of lasagne laced with walnuts and apples from one of the young men and slid his fork into the food. 'Open wide,' he said, his voice throbbing sexily. 'Open, Meredith,' he breathed.

The mask made him seem menacing, and she suddenly had the sensation that with Lucenzo she was playing with fire. He'd schooled himself to ruthlessness, single-mindedly forcing his way through the jungle, hacking at anything in his path. He would scythe her down if she didn't fit in with his plans.

She trembled from her head to her toes. Because she was hungry, she obeyed, feeling a tingle of excitement within her to have the sexually dangerous Lucenzo so close and at her feet. He had settled himself comfortably on the floor, to the astonished glances of some guests, her beautiful skirts rustling as he leant against them.

'People will talk!' she whispered.

'So they will,' he said calmly, eating some of her food and arrogantly dispatching someone to fetch another dish.

'What are you up to?' she frowned, wishing she could see his face. There were disadvantages to masked men, she thought irritably.

'Your third plate of starters, I think,' he murmured. 'Try this one. It's wonderful.'

'Ambrosia,' she agreed, trying to keep the conversation light.

'*Canastrelli*,' he corrected. Flashlights popped. Lucenzo turned, his hand familiarly on Meredith's knee. 'Smile,' he said, his voice indicating that he was certainly grinning like a Cheshire cat.

She glowered at the television crew who were filming them, but realised they had no idea she was grimacing ferociously, so she returned to sipping champagne through the straw. Her glass empty, she accepted another from Lucenzo.

'I'm supposed to be meeting your family incognito,' she complained. 'I won't impinge at all on their consciousness if I spend all night being force-fed by you.'

'Ah, the most beautiful woman in Venice.' A tall, thin man bowed low before her, and Lucenzo jumped up immediately.

'Princess, this is Jules De Vere. He's a friend of mine—a master goldsmith.'

The Frenchman ruthlessly forced the young bloods

on the couch to make room for him beside her. 'I am honoured to meet you, the brightest gem here.'

She listened to his compliments, feeling a little uncomfortable. Lucenzo had disappeared for a moment, and she wasn't too happy about the way the Frenchman was holding her hand until she realised he was harmless. He began to sing Lucenzo's praises, and she paid more attention.

'You said his bank deals in gold?' she asked, fascinated. His family and the Corosinis were linked by gold.

Jules took a piece of *pandoli* and chewed contentedly on the long biscuit. 'What else would a sensualist like Lucenzo be involved in?' he laughed. 'We both love to work with gold. It is as remarkable as a woman. When it is hot it is soft in the hands, but,' he said wickedly, 'it can be malleable if it is cold too, and you know how to handle it.'

She laughed in pure delight at his cleverness. 'You must be very rich if your skill is as remarkable as your tongue,' she told him in amusement, taking a handkerchief from her lacy sleeve to dab at a tiny droplet of champagne on her dress.

'Is something the matter, princess?' he asked, seeing that Meredith was staring at the handkerchief in consternation.

'No. Nothing,' she mumbled. 'Please go on.'

Jules continued to chatter while her mind digested the fact that she was holding Lucenzo's handkerchief—yet the initials on it were LC. Her eyes caught the Corosini crest on her plate. It was the same as the monogram on the handkerchief. Her spine chilled. Lucenzo Corosini.

Aghast behind her disguise, she nodded dumbly to Jules's chatter. Lucenzo was Corosini, she kept saying to herself. That was why he had been so hostile at the beginning, why he'd known all about the family. And he owned Isola Corosini. This was his house.

And he was her cousin.

Jules danced with her. She chatted for a long time to a friendly Madame Pompadour, who professed to love Wales and bombarded her with intimate questions. But she was in a daze, her eyes constantly seeking Lucenzo, trying to excuse and explain his lies to her own satisfaction. That was impossible, because the heat and the champagne made her feel dizzy, till she felt she could hardly concentrate. Something important was eluding her, and until she'd worked out what it was she didn't want to demand an explanation from him.

Then dimly she heard voices shouting, a gong being beaten. All faces turned to Lucenzo, who stood on a chair, his arms held out in a command for silence. He spoke in Italian, but his words were interspersed with English too, and Meredith sensed the excitement in him, her muddled brain recognising that he was about to announce something important. She went rigid with nerves.

'. . .my dear brother Rizzi and his engagement to Contessa Katarina Vivarini. . .'

The whole room burst into an uproar of approval, and Meredith found herself clapping and laughing, pleased that there was nothing more sinister.

Only Madame Pompadour beside her was motionless, and Meredith shot her a startled look when she whispered under her breath, 'Lucenzo, Lucenzo,' in a voice of infinite disappointment.

His mother, thought Meredith in panic. It must be his mother! She'd hoped Katarina would marry Lucenzo.

'Silenzio!' bellowed Lucenzo. 'Allora. . .the engagement between myself——'

An amazed buzz ran around the ballroom. The room swam before her. He meant to hurt her, to have his revenge for the trouble she and her family had caused. He'd made her love him purely so that he could reject her in public. He would jilt her, as her father had jilted Luigi's wife—that had been his mission.

'*Ecco*! Meredith!' Lucenzo cried exultantly. 'Meredith Corosini!'

He pointed directly at her. Everyone stared, their blank, featureless masks almost macabre. She felt her mouth dry up, and she would have fallen if two young men hadn't taken charge of her and marched her unprotestingly through the cheering crowd.

She flung a petrified look back at his mother. She was clapping, her hands held high as if in triumph, laughter and tears on her unmasked face. 'What's going on?' she asked hysterically when she stood before Lucenzo.

'Meredith,' he said fondly, 'you look pole-axed.' To a slow hand-clap, he slowly removed his mask and then hers, took her gently in his arms and kissed her tenderly.

'I must talk to you,' she breathed, half in despair. 'Somewhere private. . .'

'Of course,' he smiled. 'You're going to be angry with me and then we'll agree it was the only way to strike against any possible opposition. Was it a lovely surprise?'

'I—I'm stunned. Lucenzo——'

'You want to scold me,' he said understandingly. 'Let's get it over with.'

'Meredith,' came Madame Pompadour's warm voice. 'I am delighted. Welcome to our family.'

'Delighted?' she said, bewildered. 'But. . .'

'Mamma, excuse us. We have things to say to one another.' Lucenzo ruthlessly hurried the shaken Meredith through a small door, to the sound of indulgent ribaldry, and drew her into a small *salotto*. Despite her vehement protests, he hauled her enfeebled body inside and turned, laughing with delight.

She lifted a hand to her head, pushing the wig off, everything a little foggy for a moment. 'I think I need to sit down,' she whispered. 'The champagne. . .'

'Oh, sweetheart!' he groaned. 'I never thought to warn you! It's so much more potent through a straw!

Here.' She sank to the bed and leaned heavily against Lucenzo. He began to unlace her bodice, and her hands attempted to stop him in vain. 'You need to breathe, sweetheart,' he said gently. 'Doesn't it feel better?' he husked.

She felt his fingers touching her flesh, and nodded. 'Much,' she mumbled, her head spinning. But she was sure that was from the presence of the wickedly sensual Lucenzo, not the champagne. In the distance she could hear the soporific music. She must be tired, for a delicious languor was stealing over her.

'Your mother. . .' she frowned, trying to make out why she had such a sense of foreboding.

'I've taken the matter out of her hands. She knows I'm crazy about you, because I told her. She also knows I always get what I want,' he said softly. 'She adores me. Whatever I want, she wants, and she's pleased at how things have turned out. Very pleased.' He pressed his finger to his mouth, kissed it, and transferred the kiss to the centre of her cleavage.

'And me?' she asked shakily. 'Don't you care that you deceived me?' Her throat hurt. She sipped at a glass of water, wishing she knew why she was so very afraid. Outwardly she was remarkably composed, despite the pain eating away inside her. If she ever let go of her control, she'd go crazy. Scream at him, hit him. . .'Why pretend your name was Salviati, when it's Corosini?'

He went white, and her fears increased. 'When did you know that?' he asked tightly.

'About two hours ago,' she answered evenly. He relaxed a little. 'I saw the initials on your handkerchief.'

'I see.' He rose and began to prowl the room.

'I don't.'

'Sweetheart, Salviati is my true father's name. I call myself Lucenzo Salviati Corosini.'

'Luigi adopted you,' she mused. 'But there's no blood relationship between us?'

'None. I have no Corosini blood——'

'Gran demanded a share of the Corosini money for me,' she said, piecing it all together, bit by bit, 'because I'm the only descendant.'

Lucenzo stopped in his tracks and turned to examine her icy face. His eyes narrowed dangerously. 'I thought you could handle this——'

'Go on,' she said, without expression. 'Tell me why you tried to prevent me from finding out that I was a Corosini.'

His white teeth dug into his lower lip. 'I admit that the family wanted to keep you in the dark. We were expecting a man, don't forget. We thought he'd burst in and take away everything we had—everything I'd worked for so long and so hard, and he didn't deserve any of it. I had to prevent that. My duty was to those I loved.'

'Yet you changed your mind.'

'No. You changed my mind.' He looked her straight in the eyes. 'I began to realise that you had wonderful qualities, though I had to convince my mother with something more than my own feelings and impressions. So I put you through a series of tests.'

She blinked. And was astonishingly composed. 'I beg your pardon?'

'It was the only way. I had to find out a lot of things about you in a short space of time. Your honesty, for instance. You handed me back that money, remember? You proved to me that you weren't a gold-digger, that you could organise big functions, that your morals were, unfortunately, impeccable——'

'You monster!' she cried, jumping up, quivering with fury. 'You put me through a series of hoops——'

'For your own sake. You don't know what awaits you,' he said in a placatory tone, striding towards her.

'Stop right there!' she commanded, her red hair flashing in a tumble of angry waves. 'You tested me as if I were some wretched little circus dog at the

Carnival, doing tricks to please you? Am I to get a Bonio as a reward?'

Lucenzo's eyes were hard, his face turned to cold marble as if he knew he'd lost her. 'I saw no other way of protecting the interests of the Corosini,' he growled.

'I *am* the Corosini!' she said proudly. 'I'm the only real one left! Keep your wretched island and your house! I never wanted them. . .' Her voice trailed away. There was something that didn't fit. Some reason why he was watching her cautiously as if she would erupt with anger. Inside, she trembled continuously.

'You will.' He frowned at her. 'I'd better tell you. Sit down.'

'I won't——'

'*Sit down!*' he roared. Her legs took the decision from her, buckling so quickly that she stumbled back to the bed. 'This is why I had to be so careful, Meredith,' he said tightly. 'I pulled the Corosini out of debt by making the bank viable again. It belongs to Antonio's heir. You. And the palazzo on the Grand Canal—where you and I first stayed—which has almost been restored.'

'You said that didn't belong to your family.'

'It doesn't. It belongs to Antonio's heir. You. Also the estates near Padua which Rizzi manages, a stud which Fonzi runs, this island, this house. It's quite an empire, Meredith, and I created it—though I wasn't expecting to part with it, except to my son. But you have the blood and so you've inherited a fortune.'

She'd been listening to him with dawning realisation, an icy sensation freezing her body inch by inch. And suddenly she wasn't confused any longer. Her brain was crystal-clear.

'I see,' she whispered miserably. 'And when you couldn't get rid of me you worked on me as if you were working gold, moulding me to what you wanted—a malleable piece of property worth a fortune, sitting nicely in the palm of your hand.'

'No, it wasn't——'

'It was like that,' she said quietly. 'You knew I was unworldly and naïve, and you were clever enough to know how to appeal to me: through children, through my longing for family, my sexual inexperience. Then you told me what I wanted to hear: that you loved me. But it was a lie, as is everything about you. I am Antonio's heir. If you marry me, you control the Corosini wealth. I'm right, aren't I?'

'I have business interests of my own——' he began hoarsely.

'But none as special to you as those of your adoptive family. Whereas, if you become my husband, you and Rizzi and Fonzi won't be affected by my arrival,' she said, her white lips barely moving.

'Correct.' His dark eyes challenged hers.

She looked down and stared at her hands, willing herself to hold on to her sanity. He didn't love her. He'd pretended to, in order to keep the power, his position—even his title.

'You said you'd do anything for your family. You promised you'd hurt me, that you wanted everything. That at least was true,' she whispered bitterly. 'You wrote the letter to Gran! You made her die——'

'No, Meredith! No!' he roared. 'You said she was frail. I am deeply sorry for what happened, but she had caused us all terrible unhappiness and worry.'

'So you wanted to take your revenge on her grand-daughter. To trick her into a marriage of convenience,' she accused. 'What sacrifices you're prepared to make!'

'It wouldn't be a sacrifice,' he cried fiercely.

'Don't lie to me any more!' she raged, despair lending her anger a malicious knife. 'Keep some of your dignity! You couldn't bear the thought of a chit of a girl sweeping in and scooping the jackpot. So you and your family hatched a plot whereby you flirted with her and turned her stupid, innocent head; where you pawed her and manoeuvred her into private corners until she didn't know what was happening to her! And all the time the only thing that was going on was a cruel deception.'

'You can't think I'd stoop to that!' he said savagely.

'I can. You once let out the fact that you wished you were free of the burdens your family placed on you. Well, I'm relieving you of one.' She wriggled out of his astonished grasp and headed for the door.

'What are you doing?' he whispered, his face chalk-white.

'Leaving you,' she said haughtily.

'You can't!' he whispered. 'They're expecting us to return. They're imagining we're making love——'

'Well, they couldn't be more wrong, could they?' she said coldly. 'Goodbye, Lucenzo.'

'Meredith!' he said sharply. 'I do want to marry you——'

'Just because the whole of Venice is in a headlong flight from reality, it doesn't mean that you have to act stupidly. Oh, you'll find someone else. You've already perfected the tests.'

Seeing he was rooted to the spot, she swept out proudly—and bumped into Rizzi and Katarina. They were looking into each other's eyes with a tenderness that brought her a cruel, twisting anguish. This is love, she thought. This is what I wanted.

'Meredith,' smiled Rizzi. 'I'm so pleased for you—for us all.'

'Are you?' she queried jerkily.

'You look shell-shocked,' grinned Rizzi. He hugged Katarina affectionately. 'So's Kati. Everything has turned out so well. With you and Cenzo together, our family will be as solid as a rock.'

She kept her eyes lowered. All she could think of was that they'd all been in on this—a kind of family Mafia, working behind the scenes to make sure that Lucenzo ended up with everything, his empire untouched.

'My child!'

Meredith groaned. Lucenzo's mother had emerged from the ballroom and was embracing her as if she was very precious. Which she was, she supposed. From beneath her lashes she saw Lucenzo, hovering in the doorway to the *salotto*, his face impassive.

'She's quite a catch, isn't she?' grinned Rizzi.

Both Meredith and Lucenzo winced.

'Perfect!' enthused his mother. 'We feared a run on the bank when Cenzo told us you were coming. And,' she said confidingly, patting Meredith's cold face, 'we almost despaired when he said you were determined to find out everything there was to know about your family. I'm glad you're marrying my darling Cenzo and we needn't have any secrets from one another. I particularly want to hear all about your father,' she added, her voice gentle.

'How can you forgive him for leaving you?' asked Meredith bluntly.

'I have love in my life—my sons.'

Out of the corner of her eye, Meredith saw Lucenzo fold his arms, and she felt the tension in his body transfer to hers. 'Then I wish you well of them,' said Meredith. 'Because I'm not marrying Lucenzo for your convenience.'

'*What*?' breathed his mother. 'Meredith, you can't mean this! You must!'

'Why must I?' she asked angrily. 'To keep the Corosini fortune intact? You all look sick,' she scorned. 'I'll put your minds at rest. I'm not vindictive, like you. I'm leaving Venice itself.'

'What do you mean, leaving Venice?' growled Lucenzo.

'I'm going home. You can have the lot,' she snapped crisply. 'The palaces, the estates in Padua and especially the stud. You need to learn about good breeding. Because I have it, whether it's anything to do with my aristocratic ancestors or the fact that I was brought up properly in the old-fashioned way to respect integrity and honesty and decency. Keep the gondola, the mask too. I want nothing to do with you, or the Corosini—*nothing.*'

Leaving them all stunned, she walked out to the lounging boatmen, where she commandeered a motor-boat. Behind her she heard a yell, and urged the boatman on, over the dark, sinister lagoon.

The snow drifted down, muffling the sounds of the party, the fireworks spluttering, falling damply into the dark night. She could see the wash of her own boat, white in the black lagoon, and the crystal curve of Lucenzo's boat cleaving through the water at a terrifying rate. He was angry enough to harm her, she thought in panic. And if he did there would be no barrier to his inheritance.

'Faster!' she cried to the boatman piteously.

They had to make a diversion around the giant firework display in the middle of St Mark's basin, the noise of the rockets like gunfire. But they reached the shore a few moments before Lucenzo. Heedless of her full skirts, Meredith leapt out and ran through the singing, celebrating crowds, sobbing with fear and the awful sickening loss of the man she'd loved and respected. Finding your idol had feet of clay was almost unbearable, she thought miserably, darting into a narrow alley.

'Got you!'

'Ohhh!'

'Damn you, Meredith!' he growled savagely, pressing her against the wall.

'I'm going home!' she cried obstinately.

'You have no money with you,' he pointed out.

'I'm sure you'll lend me some,' she snapped, tipping up her stubborn chin.

'You, borrow money? You must be desperate,' he growled.

'I am.'

'You have no clothes. All your things are on Isola Corosini.'

'Send them,' she whispered. 'You can afford the

postage now. Lucenzo, let me go! You do want to get rid of me, don't you?'

He lifted her up on to the parapet of a little bridge, and she screamed, looking down at the dark water below. 'No,' he said wearily. 'I'm not going to throw you in. I'm just keeping you here while I force you to listen to me.'

'I won't,' she said defiantly.

He slammed his body into hers, bending her back, kissing her so hard that she fought for breath. He murmured words of adoration, lying, treacherous words, while her body responded with equal treachery, melting into his like a figure into the night. His mouth ground down hard, forcing a terrible anger to her heart because he was untrue and yet she still loved and needed him.

His mouth abruptly left hers. 'What do my lips tell you?'

'That you're cruel——'

He tried again, tenderly possessing her mouth, teasing, tormenting. 'What do they tell you?' he asked hoarsely.

'You're determined to make your shaky position legal——'

Again. And again, he kissed, he demanded the same question, he kissed and interrogated her, till she was weak with longing and he was shuddering with desire.

'You're blind, Meredith,' he said eventually. 'And I can't stand any more of this. I love you. Utterly, desperately, blindly. If you're leaving Venice, then so will I.'

She blinked. 'What?'

'Now you're listening,' he said in relief. 'Meredith, you misjudge me. It's not what you are and what you own that I care about. Sweetheart, I told Mother I was falling in love with you long before we went to the island. She made me promise that I wouldn't tell you who I was until you said you loved me. It was important that you loved *me*, not Prince Lucenzo

Corosini, and I didn't want you to think I was marrying you to strengthen my position.'

'She was so unbelievably exultant when you announced we were to marry,' muttered Meredith sulkily.

He kissed her in exasperation. 'Only because she could see I was crazy about you. She loves me. She wants me to be happy. She doesn't care who I marry, only that I'm in love. And I am.'

'How can I be sure?' she mumbled.

'You can't. So if I can't have you here, if you're determined to leave Venice, then I'm coming with you. I'll camp outside your cottage and beat on your door night and day till it finally gets into your stupid, dense head that I love you.'

'I don't——' She found herself faltering, wishing, hoping, and wondered if she was being stupid. Dense. 'You'd leave Venice?'

'Yes. I used to think your father had been a fool to go,' murmured Lucenzo. 'No, more than that—a man who lacked the guts to face up to his responsibilities. Now I know I was wrong. It takes guts to break away from the ties that bind you. I'm doing it. You're that important to me. OK. Let's go to the airport.'

'You'd live in a small cottage in Wales?' she gasped.

'Of course. If I could be your husband.' There was a sudden silence, the crowds, the music, the fireworks all still. 'It's almost midnight,' smiled Lucenzo. 'The end of Fat Tuesday. I'm unmasked. This is me, Meredith. The man who loves you. Am I to put on sackcloth and ashes?'

'What would you do?'

'Anything,' he said simply. 'Who cares, if I'm with you?'

Inside, she smiled. But she didn't let him see, keeping her face as unresponsive as if she wore her mask still. The bronze Moors were hammering out the hours on the clock in the Piazza San Marco. 'Which way to the airport?' she asked.

'This way,' he answered huskily, beginning to move over the bridge.

'No!' she said in ringing tones.

Lucenzo stiffened and whirled on his heel, his body trembling. 'Oh, God!' he groaned. 'Don't do this to me. Meredith, I love you! Is this your revenge? You'll ruin my life if I have to live with this tearing need I have for you! If you've ever had any love for me at all——'

'I have,' she breathed. 'That's why I'm not letting you take me to the airport.' His face went rigid and she couldn't bear to see his misery any longer. He loved her, he truly did. He'd been prepared to give up everything for her: Venice, his family, all he'd achieved. . . She went weak at the thought.

Her head spun dizzily with sheer joy and her face lit with her golden smile. 'Oh, Lucenzo!' she cried blissfully. 'You've proved your love for me. We'll be together, us, our family. . .children of our own.'

Dimly she heard the crowds cheering. But only dimly, since she was wrapped in Lucenzo's arms, and he was madly kissing her face and muttering loving words, holding her as if he never intended to let her go, his face now showing all he felt for her; his undying love.

'I love you, my darling. *Ti amo*. No more secrets. We begin our own fairy-tale.'

'Happy ever after,' she whispered, gazing into his eyes. Happy ever after.

VENICE—'the Queen of the Adriatic'

Breathtaking, elegant, charming, exhilarating—Venice is all these things and more. Indeed it is a city of such variety and contrasts that you will find yourself experiencing all manner of emotions as you absorb the myriad sights and sounds. It is a perfect setting for lovers, who can combine sightseeing with romantic gondola trips along the Grand Canal and moonlit walks along the maze of winding alleyways. . . Whatever your mood, Venice has something to offer for everyone.

THE ROMANTIC PAST

Venice was referred to as the **Serenissima Republic** for a thousand years, at one time ruling over a quarter of the Roman Empire, and the wealth accumulated at the height of her greatness helped to cushion her decline during the Middle Ages.

Legend has it that the original inhabitants of the city materialised from the mists and dew on the banks of the lagoon!

In the 12th century at festival time it was traditional for young Venetian men decorated in twigs and fur to wander the streets of the city with musical instruments serenading their sweethearts. This custom was later known as the **Egg Game** (*Giuoco dell Uovo*) whereby the men would dress up as devils, go to the homes of their beloveds and throw perfume-filled eggshells at them!

On April 25th at the *Festa di San Marco* it is customary for men to give Venetian girls a rosebud—a tradition that has its origin in legend. As a young Venetian fell dying after being wounded in a battle against the Turks he plucked a single white rosebud from the bush by his side for his beloved in Venice. As if by magic, after his death the flower, having been dyed with his heart's blood, was received by his lady-love in the city.

One of **Casanova's** favourite rendezvous was in the area of the **Campo dei Santi Giovanni e Paolo**, from where he would take his mistress to an apartment near the San Moisè theatre. It was some time before Casanova found out that for the duration of the affair his mistress's other lover—a future Cardinal—had been spying on him through a peephole!

Venice has been visited by a host of famous people including artists **Titian**, **Bellini**, **Tintoretto**, **Michelangelo**, **Manet**, **Renoir**; composers **Vivaldi**, **Liszt**, **Wagner**, and several literary figures—**Robert Browning**, **Lord Byron**, **Charles Dickens**, **Henry James** and **Ernest Hemingway** to name but a few.

THE ROMANTIC PRESENT—pastimes for lovers. . .

There is so much to see and do in Venice that you will be spoilt for choice, and for those of you who like to explore it's a treat. But with so much on offer and so many interconnecting alleys and streets you might prefer to arm yourself with a good map and head for the main attractions. . .

The **Grand Canal** is over 3km long and flows through the heart of the city. It is flanked by more than 200 palaces which date from the 14th to the 18th centuries, many of which are well worth a visit. The domed **Santa Maria della Salute** is a fine example of 17th century baroque architecture, while **Palazzo Pesaro** houses the **Gallery of Modern Art** and a **Museum of Oriental Art**. **Palazzo Venier dei Leone** (the name is derived from the fact that the Venier family were known to keep lions in their garden!) contains Peggy Guggenheim's collection of modern art administered by the Guggenheim Museum of New York. Arguably the most beautiful palace is the splendid **Ca'd'Oro**—renowned for its golden façade. Without a doubt Venice is a place for art lovers—be sure not to miss the **Accademia**, which has the most impressive collection of Venetian paintings in the world.

Piazza San Marco is a central feature of Venice and a great place to stop for a drink at one of its outdoor cafés—if you're feeling extravagant try **Florian's** or **Quadri's**, where you can relax and watch the world go by in style. The square is overlooked by the glorious basilica of **St Mark's**, which is filled with gold, silver, jewels and mosaics—if you enjoy being surrounded by riches, this is the place for you!

If it's views you're after, why not head for the **Rialto Bridge**, with its fine panorama over the **Grand Canal**? Or take a *vaporetto* (water-bus) to the island of **San Giorgio** where the 16th-century Palladian church has a bell tower with a lift to take you up so that you can appreciate one of the finest views of Venice without any exertion!

When your head is spinning with palaces, museums, paintings and architecture perhaps it's time for a trip by boat to one of the three main islands just a stone's throw from Venice. You can visit a glass factory at **Murano** or the lace museum at **Burano**—a lace-making centre since the 16th century. Or savour the tranquillity of **Torcello**—the perfect place to catch your breath and take a leisurely stroll in more rural surroundings.

Now let's go shopping! **The Mercerie**, situated between the **Piaza San Marco** and the **Rialto**, is probably the most famous shopping area in Venice. Here you will find mostly expensive boutiques and jewellers, but if you are seeking reasonably priced souvenirs make a detour to **Rialto Bridge**, where you can browse around the many booths. Typical souvenirs of Venice are carnival masks, tricorn hats, gondolas and Murano glass.

Since Venice is primarily a city for walkers, you are bound to work up a healthy appetite. If you need just a snack, why not have an *ombretta* (small glass of wine) and a *cicchetto* (savoury snack) at the counter of one of the many cafés? But when you want a more substantial meal there are several local specialities to choose from. *Risi e bisi* is a traditional dish of rice and peas and a particularly tasty meat dish is *fegato alla veneziana* (liver and onions). Fish is also plentiful—try *granseole* (local crab), *aragosta* (lobster), *and anguille* (eels roasted in a sauce). A popular side-dish is bitter red radicchio. To finish, *tiramisu* is a must for those of you with a sweet tooth. Of course no Italian meal is complete without wine—a good dry white is Soave Bianco or Verduzzo, but if you prefer red try Bardolino or Valpolicella.

DID YOU KNOW THAT. . .?

* in conjunction with neighbouring islands Murano, Burano, Torcello and Lido, Venice constitutes the largest **pedestrian area** on earth.

* there is a 5 mph **speed limit** on the canals, but few people stick to it!

* over 200,000 cats (at least 2 per person) roam the city and are well cared for by the Venetians, who even hold an annual **Festival of Cats**!

* boats, gondolas and barges are the only means of **transport** in Venice, even today.

* the Italian currency is **lire**.

* the way to say 'I love you' in Italian is '*Ti amo*'.

POSTCARDS FROM EUROPE*

HARLEQUIN PRESENTS*

Hi—

Have arrived safely in Germany, but Diether von Lössingen denies that he's the baby's father. Am determined that he shoulder his responsibilities!

Love, Sophie

P.S. Diether's shoulders are certainly wide enough.

Travel across Europe in 1994 with Harlequin Presents. Collect a new Postcards From Europe title each month!

Don't miss
DESIGNED TO ANNOY
by Elizabeth Oldfield
Harlequin Presents #1636

Available in March wherever Harlequin Presents books are sold.

HPPFE3

MEN. MADE IN AMERICA

**Fifty red-blooded, white-hot, true-blue hunks
from every State in the Union!**

Look for MEN MADE IN AMERICA! Written by some of our most poplar authors, these stories feature fifty of the strongest, sexiest men, each from a different state in the union!

Two titles available every other month at your favorite retail outlet.

In March, look for:

TANGLED LIES by Anne Stuart (Hawaii)
ROGUE'S VALLEY by Kathleen Creighton (Idaho)

In May, look for:

LOVE BY PROXY by Diana Palmer (Illinois)
POSSIBLES by Lass Small (Indiana)

You won't be able to resist MEN MADE IN AMERICA!

HARLEQUIN®

PRESENTS *plus*

Meet Reece Falcon. He's the elusive businessman who shows Diana Lamb that a fine line separates love and hate. He's the man who destroyed her father's life!

And then there's Leith Carew. The handsome Australian forms an awkward alliance with Suzanne after a lost child and a chance meeting bring them together. Can they possibly discover a shining love in the heart of the outback?

Reece and Leith are just two of the sexy men you'll fall in love with each month in Harlequin Presents Plus.

Watch for
ELUSIVE OBSESSION by Carole Mortimer
Harlequin Presents Plus #1631

and

THE SHINING OF LOVE by Emma Darcy
Harlequin Presents Plus #1632

Harlequin Presents Plus
The best has just gotten better!

Available in March wherever Harlequin Books are sold.

My Valentine

1994

Celebrate the most romantic day of the year with
MY VALENTINE 1994
a collection of original stories, written by
four of Harlequin's most popular authors...

MARGOT DALTON
MURIEL JENSEN
MARISA CARROLL
KAREN YOUNG

Available in February, wherever
Harlequin Books are sold.

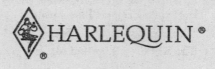

HARLEQUIN ®

VAL94

When the only time you
have for yourself is...

Spring into spring—by giving yourself a March
Break! Take a few *stolen moments* and treat yourself to a Great Escape. Relax with one of our brand-
new stories (or with all six!).

Each STOLEN MOMENTS title in our
Great Escapes collection is a complete and never-
before-published *short* novel. These contemporary
romances are 96 pages long—the perfect length
for the busy woman of the nineties!

**Look for Great Escapes in our
Stolen Moments display this March!**

SIZZLE by Jennifer Crusie
ANNIVERSARY WALTZ
by Anne Marie Duquette
MAGGIE AND HER COLONEL
by Merline Lovelace
PRAIRIE SUMMER by Alina Roberts
THE SUGAR CUP by Annie Sims
LOVE ME NOT by Barbara Stewart

**Wherever Harlequin and
Silhouette books are sold.**

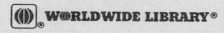 **WORLDWIDE LIBRARY®**

SMGE

Travel across Europe in 1994
with Harlequin Presents and...

As you travel across Europe in 1994, visiting your favorite
countries with your favorite authors, don't forget to collect
four proofs of purchase to redeem for an appealing photo
album. This photo album can hold over fifty 4"×6" pictures
of your travels and will be a precious keepsake in the years
to come!

One proof of purchase can be found in the back pages of
each POSTCARDS FROM EUROPE title...one every month
until December 1994.

To receive your gift, please fill out the information below and mail four (4)
original proof-of-purchase coupons from any Harlequin Presents
POSTCARDS FROM EUROPE title plus $3.00 for postage and handling
(check or money order—do not send cash), payable to Harlequin Books,
to: IN THE U.S.: P.O. Box 9048, Buffalo, NY, 14269-9048; IN
CANADA: P.O. Box 623, Fort Erie, Ontario, L2A 5X3.

Requests must be received by January 31, 1995.
Please allow 4–6 weeks after receipt of order for delivery.

Name: _____

Address: _____

_____

City: _____

State/Province: _____

Zip/Postal Code: _____

Account No: _____

ONE PROOF OF PURCHASE   077 KBY